THE HARDY BOYS
DETECTIVE HANDBOOK

The Hardy Boys Mystery Stories®

DETECTIVE HANDBOOK

BY

FRANKLIN W. DIXON

*In consultation with
Special Agent William F. Flynn
Federal Bureau of Investigation, Retired*

GROSSET & DUNLAP
Publishers • New York
A member of The Putnam Publishing Group

FOREWORD

Police science is one of the youngest and most rapidly growing professions in the United States today. I have revised this handbook for fans of Frank and Joe Hardy who are interested in learning about modern police practices.

The first seven chapters, based upon true stories from police files, illustrate how Frank and Joe use the various facets of police technology while tracking down criminals. Further uses of these techniques—fingerprinting, surveillance, and other related skills in the science of criminal investigation—are detailed in the last five chapters.

William F. Flynn, FBI Special Agent who recently retired, acted as my consultant in the preparation of this revised edition. It is our sincere hope that many readers of this handbook will someday join the ranks of our country's brave and dedicated law-enforcement officers who fight the never-ending war against crime.

F.W.D.

CONTENTS

THE HARDY BOYS
DETECTIVE HANDBOOK

CHAPTER I

MYSTERY OF THE VANISHING PLASTICS

Undercover Work

"Boys, I've taken on an important investigation for the Domas Plastics Company of Dover. I think you can help me."

Fenton Hardy, the famous private detective, sat behind the mahogany desk in his study and looked across at eighteen-year-old Frank and his brother Joe, who was a year younger.

"How, Dad?" dark-haired Frank asked eagerly.

"I'm convinced," Mr. Hardy went on, "that this case can be solved only by undercover work. Since you're on vacation, how would you like to be my assistants?"

"Try and stop us," Joe said with a grin.

"We were hoping something exciting would turn up this summer," Frank said.

The boys were pleased that their father had so much faith in their detective ability. Mr. Hardy had trained his sons thoroughly in police science and they had become very proficient investigators.

"When do we start?" Frank asked.

"I've already laid the plans," his father replied. "Listen to them carefully. As of tomorrow, you'll be known as Frank and Joe Ghent and will be given credentials for those names."

"Wow! Cover names and all!" Frank exclaimed.

"You'll go to the employment office of the Domas Plastics Company," Mr. Hardy continued, "and you'll be given jobs in their packing department. I've reserved accommodations for all of us in a rooming house in Dover. We'll have adjoining rooms."

"Will you be working undercover too, Dad?" Joe asked.

"Yes. I'm Jerry Ghent, your uncle. I'll be employed in the shipping room."

"Exactly what are we supposed to look for, Dad?" Frank inquired.

"I'm coming to that. Domas is a fairly large company. They make household articles and some rather expensive decorative items. Past inventories have shown small losses in finished goods, probably due to pilferage by employees. The last inventory, however, has shown a staggering loss.

"Besides this, two molds which cost the company ten thousand dollars apiece have been stolen."

"Dad," interjected Joe, "why do you want us in the packing department?"

Mr. Hardy studied a sheaf of notes. "I've a feeling that's where the action starts. A lot of Domas products, packaged as usual, are being sold all over the state under the guise of a special sale for less than the list price."

"Who sells them?" Frank asked.

"They are offered by telephone and delivered C.O.D.—cash on delivery, by various truck drivers. The physical descriptions of the men are not very conclusive."

"About those molds," Joe spoke up. "Are there any clues to them?"

"Yes. Two rival plastics companies have informed the president of Domas, Mr. Albert Matt, that they were approached by an unknown man over the telephone. He offered to sell the molds for five thousand dollars each. I have communicated with every plastics manufacturer who makes products similar to the Domas line and asked them to notify Mr. Matt in case they are contacted by anyone offering to sell the molds. All these companies have agreed to cooperate."

"Who else knows about our role in this operation?" Frank asked.

"Only Mr. Matt, George Sard, who is the plant manager, and Captain Nast of the Dover Detective Bureau."

Mr. Hardy leaned forward to emphasize his next point. "Tomorrow morning report in your work clothes to Mr. Sard. He'll be expecting you, and place each of you in one of the two packing rooms.

"From there on you'll be on your own. Keep your ears and eyes open and make a mental note of everything. Follow all the rules of undercover work and you should have no trouble."

The boys nodded.

"We'll meet at night," Mr. Hardy went on, "and compare notes. Is it all clear?"

"So far, yes," Joe replied. "We're to discover how the merchandise is disappearing and who is stealing it."

"Exactly, son."

"And," Frank put in, "we must find out where the plastic molds are. It seems to me that whoever is stealing the merchandise is also involved in the theft of the molds."

"That's my deduction, too," Mr. Hardy said.

"Have you checked the background of all the personnel in the plant, Dad?" Joe asked.

"The Dover police did. They investigated everyone from the president down to the porters. But since all the members of the police department are likely to be known to the thieves, I was called in to do the undercover work."

Mr. Hardy paused, then went on. "Domas needs few skilled workers. They've been hiring a number of unskilled employees. Most of the routine jobs are done by them. The key workers are older, skilled machinists who make the molds and work the presses. Then there are about twenty younger men, mostly unskilled. They do the heavy work, including packing and shipping.

"It's in the last group that four have criminal

records," Mr. Hardy continued. "At this point, all employees are suspect, but I think these deserve special attention. Have a look." He handed his sons four dossiers.

Frank and Joe examined the material as carefully as if studying for a final exam. They memorized the men's outstanding physical characteristics and inspected their criminal records minutely. Finally they placed the folders before their father.

"Well," Mr. Hardy said with a smile, "let's see what you've learned about these characters. Which one served a sentence in Sing Sing?"

"Alexander Smathers," the boys replied simultaneously.

"Joe," the detective went on, "tell me all you can remember about him."

Joe drew a deep breath. "Smathers has the worst criminal record of all. He was born in Brooklyn, is five-feet four-inches tall, weighs one hundred and forty-five pounds, has gray eyes, large nose, wavy brown hair, dresses flashily, is a bachelor and likes to gamble. He is a fast talker, has small, close-set eyes, good teeth, seldom smiles, moves and walks quickly. He'll be easy to recognize, Dad."

"Frank, has Joe left anything out?"

"He forgot the age, which is thirty-seven. Smathers' long record shows convictions for assault and battery, grand larceny, burglary and embezzlement."

"I knew that, but forgot to mention it," Joe said sheepishly.

Mr. Hardy nodded, then said to Frank, "Tell us what you've learned about Sam Streeter."

"He's thirty years old, five-feet eleven-inches tall, weighs one hundred and ninety pounds, was born in Cleveland. He has spent most of his life in New York. He has brown eyes, low forehead, black hair, big mouth, large protruding ears, square jaw, poor teeth, and moves slowly."

Frank hesitated a moment. "Oh, yes. He has a poor education, is not very intelligent, dresses in work clothes or sport clothes, and is not married. He has a long record of convictions for grand larceny. I guess that's about all."

"Have you anything to add?" Mr. Hardy asked Joe.

"Only that Streeter smokes cigars. He seems to have one in his mouth all the time and chews on it."

"Let's go on from here," said Mr. Hardy, obviously pleased. "Frank, tell us about Harry Rands."

"Rands is twenty-two. He was born in New York City, is single, has a long juvenile record for assault and battery, purse snatchings, burglary and larceny. He has two convictions as an adult, for auto thefts and grand larceny. It also seems that he will resort to violence at the slightest provocation, mainly because he is strong and muscular. He is five-feet ten-inches tall, weighs one hundred and eighty pounds, has brown eyes, brown wavy hair, fair complexion.

"Rands graduated from high school. He has a nervous habit of cracking his fingers and laughs loudly at the smallest jokes. That's all that's important, I guess."

"How about the last character?" inquired Mr. Hardy, looking at Joe quizzically.

"Let's review the rules about undercover work,"
said Mr. Hardy

"His name is Edward Cowell and his nickname is Slick. A convicted thief; he is twenty-three years old, about five-feet six-inches, weighs one hundred and forty pounds, has long black hair, brown eyes, and a small flat nose. Cowell blinks his eyes continually. He is sarcastic and always ready with a wisecrack."

"Very good," said Mr. Hardy. "Now let's review the rules about undercover work. Joe, you begin."

"Okay. An undercover operator is one who changes his character so that he can associate with criminals and obtain information necessary to an investigation and—"

"You mean he's got to be a good actor!" interjected Frank.

"That's right." His father nodded.

"As I was saying before I was interrupted," Joe continued with a smile, "an undercover operator must be intelligent and possess initiative. He should be courageous and cool at all times."

"Very good," Mr. Hardy said. "Now, Frank, since you seem so eager to get into this act, tell us something about the preparations for an undercover agent."

"That's easy. First, he must know exactly what information he's looking for. Next, he learns the best character to assume under the circumstances and plays that role so well he actually becomes the character.

"He must dress the part and use the kind of speech expected from him. He learns to anticipate every possible question that he may be asked and give predetermined answers whenever possible. How's that?"

"Frank, you forgot a couple of things," Joe stated. "An agent working undercover must never carry any incriminating papers, letters, badges, or other articles that may reveal his true identity. He makes it his business to create situations where he may meet, talk to, and become familiar with those persons from whom he is seeking information. In the Domas case we'll be working with them and probably eating at the same places. Right, Dad?"

"Correct. Now what have we left out?"

"Communications with headquarters," Frank replied. "But the reason I didn't bring it up is that we won't have that problem. You'll be there in the same rooming house with us."

"Let's review it anyway, in the event our plans should change," said the detective.

"Okay, here goes," Frank volunteered. "Every agent must communicate with headquarters or another agent acting as a go-between. He must memorize all telephone numbers he might have to call, or addresses he might have to write to. He can't take chances and carry written telephone numbers or addresses around. If he has an appointment to meet another agent, he must choose the location carefully and exercise caution going to and from it. If he is followed, it means failure."

Mr. Hardy added solemnly, "The revelation that an agent is working undercover has sometimes meant his death. So, boys, be careful. Here are identification papers made out in your new names. We will try to stick as close to the true story of your lives as possible. You were both born in Bayport and attended school here. Your father died when you were young.

"The reason you came to work for Domas was because you have been thrown out of school after being in trouble with the police many times and—"

"What kind of trouble?" interrupted Frank.

"Well, let's not make you too bad," replied Mr. Hardy with a grin. "Just a few arrests for burglary, purse snatching, and a car theft. That's a typical juvenile delinquency pattern."

"Wow!" exclaimed Frank, looking at Joe. "We sure are a couple of hoods!"

Next day the young detectives presented themselves at the Domas Plastics Company and were immediately hired. Joe was to work in packing room designated as Number 1, and Frank in Number 2. The first day was uneventful, marked by little conversation between themselves and their co-workers. Both realized that they were subjected to stares of curiosity by their colleagues.

That night the three Hardys met in the detective's room to review their activities. "I'm certain you didn't learn much today," Mr. Hardy said. "That's to be expected. But I hope you've been thinking about the possible ways in which those thefts are being made."

"Joe and I talked about it after work," Frank said. "We cased the layout. Both packing rooms are alike, except in size. No one but employees of the packing and shipping departments are allowed to enter. So far we have no idea who steals the stuff and how. Seems like a tough case, Dad."

The detective looked at his son severely. "You're forgetting your role! Call me Uncle Jerry at all times!"

"Sorry, er—Uncle Jerry."

Joe said, "I recognized Harry Rands. He works in my packing room and looks like a mean customer. All the workers seem to be afraid of him."

"Cowell is in my packing room," Frank said. "And the nickname Slick fits him like a glove. He talks to everybody in the place and moves around quickly."

"Smathers and Streeter are in the shipping department with me," Mr. Hardy added.

Frank stood up and paced around the room. "Joe and I went to the luncheonette down the street at noon," he said. "Smathers and Streeter came in. They started to play the pinball machine. Rands and Cowell joined them. They were playing for money on high scores."

"Yes!" said Joe. "And who do you think was winning most of the time?"

"Slick?"

"Right."

"By the way, Uncle Jerry," Frank said, "they looked our way a few times, probably talking about us."

"Don't worry about their curiosity," said Mr. Hardy. "But avoid becoming self-conscious and betraying yourselves."

The boys nodded.

Joe suddenly exclaimed, "I've got it! A good way to meet those guys would be to get to the luncheonette early and start playing the pinball machine while we eat our sandwiches. Maybe they'll offer to play with us."

"An excellent idea," Mr. Hardy said approvingly. "But don't overact your parts."

Next evening the three gathered again. The detective sat down in a comfortable chair and the boys lounged on his bed, looking glum.

"What happened today?" Mr. Hardy began.

"Nothing on my end," Joe replied.

"I made a little progress," Frank said. "Cowell spoke to me a few times. Asked where I was from and things like that, but I made believe I wasn't too eager to talk."

"Good. Now don't be so disappointed. You can't make much progress in a day or two."

"We can't spend months, either," Joe said. "We'll have to get back to school!"

Mr. Hardy laughed. "Don't worry. I believe we'll get a break sooner than you think. By the way, what happened to the pinball machine idea?"

Frank looked crestfallen. "I stopped to wash when the lunch-hour whistle blew, and when I reached the outside and met Joe, he told me that our friends had already gone into the luncheonette. I guess they didn't stop to clean up."

"The moral of this story is, don't be too clean. I suggest you go to lunch promptly tomorrow."

Next evening Joe started the conversation. "Nothing important happened today, except that we did beat them to the pinball machine. When they filed in and saw us playing, our suspects gave us black glances and whispered among themselves. But none of them offered to play with us!"

"That's right," said Frank, "and I noticed that Cowell was staring at me all afternoon. I wonder if he's suspicious."

"It probably means," Mr. Hardy replied, "that he's becoming interested in you and is observing you closely. Sooner or later you'll get a break—provided you're careful."

"Uncle Jerry, I noticed one thing that may be important," said Joe. "A man came into the luncheonette and ate with our suspects. He also walked into the packing room three times during the afternoon and spoke with Cowell. One of the girls told me he's Clarence Sard, the manager's brother, who's in charge of quality control."

Mr. Hardy's eyebrows arched. "Hm! They could have been discussing business, but it's a little odd that he would have lunch with the packers. Usually the Sards eat at The Pub. I'll check this angle out tomorrow."

The next two days Frank and Joe drew a blank, and so did Mr. Hardy. But at the beginning of the second week, all were smiling when they met in the detective's room.

Joe spoke first. "Believe it or not, Rands talked to me a couple of times today. He seemed friendly."

"And Cowell was buddy-buddy with me," said Frank. "He made it his business to work near me as much as possible. At lunch he and I played pinball for a while, then Joe and Rands joined us. We played for a nickel a game and Cowell won almost every time. He surely knows how to manipulate that machine!"

"I can't understand what made them so friendly," Joe remarked.

Mr. Hardy grinned. "I might be responsible for that. I told a couple of gossipy fellows confidentially that you boys had been in trouble with the police and had served a term in reform school. Evidently the news has reached your friends!"

Frank said soberly. "There's one thing that bothers me. Smathers and Streeter never came over to the pinball machine."

"The reason," Mr. Hardy replied, "is probably because they are older and more suspicious. It will take them a while longer to accept you. Now both of you go take a walk, then go to bed. I have some thinking to do."

The next evening Frank was leaving the plant when Cowell called to him. "Wait, Frank!" The man sidled up and whispered, "What have you got in your pockets?"

Defiantly the boy answered, "None of your business!"

"I saw you take those ashtrays," Cowell said. "But I won't squeal. What are you going to do with them?"

Frank glanced left and right, then said, "I'm going to sell them. I spent all my money over the weekend and I'm broke." Nervously he added, "You're not going to report me, are you?"

"Naw. But that's only petty larceny stuff. You ought to get into the big money."

"I'm game," Frank said. "But where are you going to find big-time stuff in this joint?"

Cowell looked thoughtful, as if he had said too much. "I'm just kidding," he muttered. "Forget it. I'll see you tomorrow."

Frank waited outside the plant for Joe and told him of the conversation. Then they headed for the rooming house and went directly to their father's room. The detective arrived minutes later, and Frank relayed the information.

"That was fast thinking," Mr. Hardy said.

"I made sure Cowell saw me put the stuff into my pockets," Frank remarked.

Joe grinned. "That's how to make friends with thieves. Seems we're headed for action!"

"Good," Mr. Hardy said, and added, "Domas has been manufacturing some new products. In a week or so they should be ready for shipment. Unless we can crack this case before then, the company will begin to lose a large amount of merchandise right away."

"Uncle Jerry, you've been working close to Streeter and Smathers," Joe said. "How have they been acting lately?"

"At first they were aloof and suspicious. But the past two days they've been more friendly—even asked about you boys."

"No kidding," Frank said. "Cowell quizzes me about you, too. They're comparing our answers."

"This shows," Mr. Hardy said emphatically, "that you can't be too careful about what you say."

The three sat up late, mapping their strategy. It was agreed that if any move occurred, it would have to be through the initiative of the suspects. Frank would continue "pilfering" plastics and Joe would begin the next day.

The friendly relations among Frank, Joe, Cowell, and Rands grew during the rest of the week. They played the pinball machine at lunch and were joined by Streeter and Smathers.

On Friday, as Frank and Cowell were walking to the luncheonette, Frank said nervously, "Can you loan me a couple of bucks? I'm broke."

Laughing, Cowell pulled a wad of money from his pocket. He picked out a bill and handed it to Frank in a grand manner. "Here's a ten. Pay me when you're on the plush."

"Slick," Frank said in admiration, "that's quite a roll. You make that much money?"

Cowell chuckled. "You kidding? Nobody makes anything in this cheap outfit." He glanced about cautiously, then whispered, "Maybe I can let you in on something. Where do you live?"

Frank told him, then they were joined by Joe and Rands and the conversation ended.

As the Hardys conferred in the boys' room that evening, a knock sounded on the door. Cowell and Rands walked in.

"Hi, fellows," Cowell greeted. "Hi, Mr. Ghent! You must be keeping an eye on your nephews, huh?"

Mr. Hardy grinned. "They can pretty much take care of themselves." A general conversation followed and Mr. Hardy noted that both Rands and Cowell moved about the room casually, taking in everything. Then, apparently satisfied, Cowell suggested that Frank and Joe take a walk with him and Rands.

It was late when the boys returned, but their father had waited up for them.

"Uncle Jerry," Frank said, "they took us to a recreation hall where Smathers and Streeter were playing pool. A little later Clarence Sard came in. All of them seemed to be sizing us up."

"They asked a lot of questions," Joe added. "I think Sard is part of their group."

"You're probably right," Mr. Hardy said slowly, as if deliberating. "It wouldn't surprise me if he were

"How would you like to make some easy money?"
Cowell asked

the ringleader, even though his brother is the plant manager. We'd better watch him carefully." He yawned. "Let's get some sleep."

On Monday, as Frank and Cowell were returning to the packing room after lunch, the latter stopped and half-whispered to Frank, "How would you like to make some easy money?"

Frank appeared surprised. "I'll do anything within reason. Only whatever I do, Joe comes in with me. But my uncle must be kept in the dark."

"Suits me," rejoined Cowell. "I'll let you know when it's okay."

The following afternoon Cowell told Frank to bring Joe to the recreation hall at seven that night. When they arrived, Cowell was waiting for them in the doorway. He led them into a back room, where they found Rands, Streeter, Smathers, and Clarence Sard seated around a table.

"Okay, fellows," Cowell said. "Sit down."

Smathers opened the conversation. "Slick says you want to throw in with us, right?"

Frank nodded, while Joe responded with pretended enthusiasm, "Sure—if we get a fair cut."

Streeter said belligerently, "We're letting you kids in on this, but you'd better keep your mouths shut! Until now everything has been going along fine and we expect it to stay that way. But—"

Cowell interrupted. "Take it easy, Sam. The boys are okay. Let's get down to business."

Joe said quietly, "Frank and I've been around. You don't have to worry about us. But if you don't trust us, we'll forget about the whole deal. Let's go, Frank!" He rose from his chair.

"Wait a minute!" Smathers cut in. "Let's stop acting like kids! Sit down, Joe!"

Sard cleared his throat and began. "It's an easy racket. There's no trouble at all. This is how it goes: The girls in the office make out labels addressed to the dealers who are to receive the merchandise. The labels go to the packing rooms together with instructions of what is to be sent. The stuff is packed, the labels glued on the cartons, and then the shipping department takes care of the loading. The company uses outside truckers to make deliveries. Follow me?"

"Sure. So far," replied Frank. "But I don't see how we come in on it."

Everyone but Joe laughed, and Sard continued, "Here's how. We have labels of our own which I lifted when I had a chance. We type the address of an old warehouse on them with a typewriter we bought at a pawnshop.

"Harry and Slick pack whatever we need and put those labels on the extra packages. Then they're trucked to the warehouse by drivers who work with us."

"Pretty clever scheme," Frank put in.

"You bet," Cowell said. "In the warehouse we sort out the stuff, then pack the goods we've sold to our dealers, and arrange for delivery."

Frank and Joe gave an approving nod, and Cowell added, "We only take what we have a market for. Smart, eh?"

"That's real slick, Slick," said Joe.

There was a murmur of approval at Joe's play on words, then Sard continued. "Domas is bringing out a new line which will be shipped soon. We're going to cash in on this, and big, too!

"We'll take a truckload in the morning, and another in the afternoon."

"Won't that look funny?" queried Joe. "I mean, doesn't it seem peculiar, just loading stuff for our warehouse?"

Sam Streeter snorted, "Do you think we're that dumb? There's legitimate orders on those trucks, too."

"I guess you guys thought of everything," remarked Joe.

"We're sure glad we're in with you," Frank added.

Clarence Sard nodded. "We can use some more help." He took an envelope from his inside pocket and doled out the labels to Frank, Harry, Joe, and Slick, and told them what products to pack and how many of each.

Then the boys left, impatient to see Fenton Hardy.

When they arrived at the rooming house, the young detectives reported the latest developments to their father. They exhibited the labels. Mr. Hardy made a mental note of the address.

He looked at his sons and said quietly, "You did a great job. Keep on, but don't take any unnecessary chances. The case is as good as solved."

Frank and Joe nodded.

"I'm going to notify Captain Nast. He'll be ready for the showdown. Now go to bed and relax."

For the next few days the boys followed orders of the gang. Monday night after work there was a knock on the door of their room. Cowell walked in and invited them to take a stroll. They agreed, calling to their "uncle" that they were going out with Slick.

Outside, Cowell beckoned them to his car and slid behind the wheel.

"Where're we going?" Frank asked.

"To the warehouse," replied Slick. "Now that you're in with us, you're going to work!"

"We don't mind," Frank said. "It's better than sitting in our room, watching TV and hearing Uncle Jerry snoring."

"You'll see a swell setup," Cowell said as they stopped in front of a dilapidated warehouse. It was located in the waterfront section of the city.

They got out and Cowell gave three sharp raps on the door, paused, and then rapped once. The door opened and the boys found themselves in a large dimly lighted room crammed with Domas packages.

Streeter and Rands were moving them around, sorting them by product. Smathers had a list in his hands and was calling out the articles needed. Clarence Sard sat at a table, pecking away laboriously on a typewriter. He was preparing a new set of labels with the addresses of the dealers.

Frank noticed a padlocked closet in one corner of the room.

"What's in there?" he asked Cowell, pointing.

"None of your business," was the curt reply.

Smathers looked up and growled. "It's about time you guys pitched in. Come over here and stack up these boxes like I tell you!"

The boys joined in with alacrity, and made up various piles at Smathers' direction. From time to time, Clarence Sard mumbled and swore, remarking that the typewriter was defective. The men's bantering about his typing ability increased his anger.

Finally Frank said, "Will you let me try? I used to work in the office at reform school and learned to type a little."

Sard accepted the offer. He showed Frank the names and addresses of dealers to be typed on the labels and watched him work. Frank was careful not to type too well.

About ten o'clock Sard announced that enough work had been completed for the evening. They stood around and talked a while.

Finally Smathers said, "Clarence has made contacts to dispose of this stuff at a good price. We'll hire two trucks day after tomorrow to make the deliveries. Everybody be ready to report here to load them."

He cleared his throat, then went on, "Clarence has also made arrangements to sell those molds we have. We can't get the price we wanted, but we'd better get rid of them. They're too hot."

Streeter exulted, "It looks like we're in for a good piece of change."

The group broke up and Slick drove the boys back to their rooming house. Frank and Joe reported to their father everything that had happened. They described the warehouse minutely, including the type of locks on the doors, the padlock on the closet, and the location of the light switch on the wall.

When they mentioned the prospective sale of the molds, Mr. Hardy laughed quietly and said, "I arranged that. Right after Clarence Sard contacted the Phoenix Plastics Company, I was notified. I requested that they negotiate with him and they have done so."

The detective went on, "I'm going to slip out and meet Captain Nast to inform him of the latest developments. He'll keep a sharp watch on the warehouse until we're ready to close in."

The next evening the Hardys were again picked up by Cowell. They went to the warehouse and continued their work as on the previous night. They noticed, however, that Clarence Sard was not present.

Smathers grumbled, "I wonder what's keeping him. He should have been here half an hour ago. And he's got the list of purchasers on him."

At that instant a key turned in the lock. Clarence Sard entered and slammed the door angrily behind him. His eyes had a wild look.

"Where have you been?" Smathers demanded. "We'll never get these shipments ready for tomorrow now!"

"Where have I been?" Sard shouted. "At my brother's house." He pointed to Frank and Joe. "I found out that these kids are stool pigeons and are working for their father, Detective Fenton Hardy, who is posing as their uncle!"

The men glared at the boys in fury. Smathers pulled out a switchblade knife and advanced toward the Hardys menacingly. There were shouts and curses from the other members of the gang.

Instantly Frank and Joe separated slightly and retreated. Frank headed toward the door with Joe a few feet away from him. Suddenly Frank reached up and snapped off the light switch.

Pandemonium broke lose in the darkness, with the thieves striking out wildly in utter confusion. There were groans of pain as they mistakenly mauled one another.

Suddenly there was a loud pounding on the door and a voice called out, "This is Captain Nast. I have a search warrant!" The door was flung open and in stormed the captain, a flashlight in one hand and a pistol in the other.

"Stop where you are!" he commanded.

Right behind him were Mr. Hardy and a detective. Frank switched on the light. Smathers dropped the knife on the concrete floor.

"Raise your hands above your heads and face the wall!" Captain Nast ordered. "You're all under arrest!"

He turned to Clarence Sard and served the search warrant. Then he directed the detective to frisk the thieves.

All incriminating papers were taken from them. Within minutes four uniformed police officers were on the scene. The prisoners were handcuffed and taken to jail.

Mr. Hardy telephoned Albert Matt, president of Domas Plastics Company, and the plant manager, George Sard. Both came to the warehouse. They were amazed at the amount of merchandise stored there and identified it as having been manufactured in their plant.

Fenton Hardy walked over to the closet. He looked at the padlock, selected a key from a case of master keys, and opened the door. In it were the two plastic molds. Mr. Matt confirmed that they were the ones stolen from Domas.

All this while Frank and Joe had been staring curiously at George Sard. The manager noticed this and said with a smile, "Is anything wrong?"

Frank asked in amazement, "Don't you know that your brother Clarence was the ringleader of the gang?"

"These kids are stool pigeons!" Sard shouted

"Wh-what?"

"Tonight," Frank went on, "you told him about Joe and me doing undercover work. He came straight here and revealed our identities. If it hadn't been for Captain Nast and my father breaking in when they did, we might have been killed!"

George Sard turned white and became so weak that he had to sit down. Shaking, he said, "I invited Clarence over to dinner. He seemed very nervous. When I asked him what was the matter, he said he was concerned about the stolen molds. I told him to stop worrying. Mr. Matt had hired the famous detective Fenton Hardy, and he would find the molds. He had brought his two boys Frank and Joe to help him."

George Sard sighed. "Believe me, fellows, I never in the world had any inkling my brother was involved in the thefts."

Upon arraignment in court the next morning, the prisoners pleaded guilty to the charges filed against them by the District Attorney.

After court the Hardys and Captain Nast went to a nearby restaurant for lunch. The Dover police officer expressed his appreciation for the Hardys' work. To Frank and Joe, however, the greatest praise came from their father, who said. "Boys, you followed the rules of undercover work in this case to perfection. Congratulations!"

CHAPTER II

THE CLUE OF THE CASHBOX
Fingerprint Proof

THE telephone rang shrilly in the Hardy home.

"I'll take it," said Joe. As he hurried into the hall he called back to his brother, "Frank, get out the fingerprint kit so we can show it to Chet."

Chet Morton, the Hardys' closest friend, had asked them to teach him the science of fingerprinting.

Joe picked up the phone. "Joe Hardy speaking. . . . Oh, hi, Dad. How are you coming along on the New York case?"

"I expect to be in Bayport late tomorrow," his father replied. "But before I get back, there's an important job I want you and Frank to do for me. Dr. Gladstone just called me from Bayport at the request of Chief Collig to arrange for processing a crime scene."

"I see, Dad," broke in Joe. "He called you here . . . sounded very worried. So I gave him the number of your hotel in New York."

"He was upset," replied the detective. "His office was burglarized and twenty-seven hundred dollars in cash was stolen. I spoke to Chief Collig and he told me the Bayport police are holding a suspect, but they haven't located the stolen money."

"What do you want Frank and me to do, Dad?"

"Locate, photograph, and lift fingerprints at the scene. As you know, one of Chief Collig's fingerprint experts is here with me to testify in this case, and the other one is in the hospital with a broken wrist."

"That leaves the chief really short-handed, doesn't it?"

"Yes. Call him right away. He's expecting to hear from you."

As soon as Mr. Hardy had hung up, Joe dialed Bayport Police Headquarters. The chief said he would send a car to take the boys to the scene of the burglary. "I'm leaving for Dr. Gladstone's now and will meet you there," he added.

Frank came downstairs with the fingerprint kit and a camera just as Joe put the phone back in its cradle. He also carried a small black box.

"Boy, are we in luck!" Joe said. "Now Chet can see how a real case is handled." He told them about the theft and added, "A police car will be here shortly."

"While we're waiting, will you show me the equipment?" Chet asked.

Investigator's camera

"Sure," Frank replied. "This is an investigator's camera, sometimes called a press camera. It can be adapted to take pictures in a one-to-one ratio of visible and dusted latent fingerprints."

"Can you use other cameras, too?" Chet asked.

"Yes. However, most police departments use either the investigator's camera or one made especially for this work, commonly called a fingerprint camera."

"What's the difference?"

"The investigator's camera is more widely used because it can be employed in many other areas of police work as well as—"

"Oh, oh," Chet interrupted, "here comes the police car." But the black sedan he had seen approaching the Hardy residence continued down the street.

Joe took the camera and removed it from its case. He opened the front and extended the lens. Then he produced an angular, tapering sheet-metal trough with a ring feature attached to the small end.

"You see, Chet," he said, "the ring fits over the lens housing." He pointed to three screws protruding from the ring and added, "The trough is fastened in place with these."

"And what do you need this contraption for?" Chet wanted to know.

"It's an adapter which permits us to focus the camera so that a fingerprint will photograph in its original size."

"I see."

"This makes it easier for the expert, who will compare fingerprint photos with inked prints appearing on an arrest fingerprint card. It also helps in preparing comparable enlargements for use in court."

Chet nodded. "I understand. Now tell me about the fingerprint camera."

"Its use," Joe went on, "is basically limited to fingerprint work and photographing signatures on forged checks and documents. It's meant to be used on flat surfaces, otherwise distortions occur due to improper focus."

Frank put in, "Let me explain the construction of the fingerprint camera to Chet. It's essentially a compartmented box with a predetermined focal depth which produces only a one-to-one reproduction of the subject."

"In other words, you don't need an adapter."

"Right. The shutter is manually operated and the exposure time is determined by the operator's manipulation of the shutter. There is no lens adjustment. The camera is equipped with batteries and/or an extension cord which can be plugged into a wall outlet to provide power for built-in electric light bulbs by which variations in lighting and cross-lighting may be obtained.

"However," Frank went on, "because of the limitations Joe mentioned, many police departments believe the cost of such a specialized camera is not justified when the investigator's camera can be adapted to do the same job."

"That makes sense," Chet commented.

Frank carried on with the explanation. "In most cases, the investigator's camera will photograph a larger area, and minor adjustments in focus and lighting can be made when photographing latent fingerprints on curved or irregular surfaces. It can be used in other routine police work—accident investigations, photographing crime scenes, and taking mug shots of arrested persons."

Chet asked, "Talking about latent fingerprints, you say you dust them to make them visible?"

"Correct. There are many different colored powders on the market, but Dad says that only the black and gray ones have real practical value. You use whatever powder gives the best contrast, depending upon the color of the object. Incidentally, the powder also comes in aerosol cans and can be sprayed over a latent print. Furthermore—"

"Wait a minute," interjected Joe. "You should explain why powders are used."

"Okay. Well, Chet, all fingerprint impressions and footprints are made by ridges which appear only on the palmar areas of the hands and the soles of the feet.

Fingerprints are the markings left on objects touched by the ridges on the bulb of each finger."

He added that fingerprint experts can actually make an identification by comparing ridge detail left at a crime area with an inked impression of the same ridges, taken either from a suspect's hand or foot."

"Fingerprints are left," Joe took up the explanation, "because of tiny ducts which emit an oily substance. It's really sweat, and every time the hand or foot touches something, a little is left on the object."

Frank added that there are a few persons in the world who do not leave latent prints. "They are called nonsecreters because they do not perspire. Most people do, however. And generally young persons perspire more freely and therefore leave stronger prints than older persons. The more excited or emotional they get, the more they perspire and the stronger their prints are."

"I'm learning fast," said Chet. "Now what about the visible print?"

"That's made by an individual who has had his fingers in material like paint, blood, grease, ink, or other similar substances," Joe said.

"There's one thing I forgot to say about latent prints," Frank put in. "They're hard to locate. The best way is to shine a flashlight over the surface at an angle."

"What's in the kit?" Chet inquired.

Frank opened the lid. "We call this the Hardy Fingerprint Kit," he said. "Joe and I assembled it."

Chet noted that it contained a long-handled magnifying glass, a small two-cell flashlight, jars of black and gray powder, two camel's-hair brushes, a supply of black and white rubberized lifting tape, transparent lifting tape, and backup cards for the transparent tape. Scissors for cutting the tape to the proper size were also in the kit.

Joe said, "The rubberized tape usually comes in sheets four-by-eight inches and is similar to the tape used to repair bicycle tire punctures. One side of it is covered with a sticky substance. Over it is a transparent plastic layer."

"Now wait a minute," Chet interrupted. "What do you need that stuff for?"

"I'll get to that. Let's go step by step." Joe explained further.

1. The powders are dusted on an area thought to contain latent fingerprints.
2. The prints are made visible.
3. The prints are photographed.
4. The plastic cover on the rubber tape is removed and the tape is pressed firmly over the dusted print.
5. The tape is peeled off, bringing with it the powder.
6. The plastic cover is then replaced to seal the powder on the tape. This prevents its becoming smudged and at the same time permits the latent impression to be visible.

Chet had a question. "Do you always use powder on all surfaces?"

"No," Frank answered. "Actually there are two types of surface: porous and nonporous. On the porous, like unglazed paper, rough cardboard, and unfinished wood, the perspiration is absorbed and little powder will stick. The prints then must be developed by a chemical process. The most useful methods are iodine fuming and the application of a silver nitrate solution. Oil in the print absorbs the iodine, but the mark must be photographed at once because it fades quickly. Silver nitrate combines with the salt in perspiration, which is left along with the print, to form silver chloride. This substance darkens under strong light."

"Dusting is still the most common method for nonporous surfaces, however," Joe put in, "because the equipment is the easiest to carry around."

Frank had just started to tell how the powder is placed on the print with a camel's-hair brush, when a police sedan came to a stop in front of the house. The three boys hurried to the car. Officer Con Riley was at the wheel. Frank slid in beside him, while Joe and Chet jumped into the back seat.

As they drove off, Riley remarked, "Looks as if this is an open-and-shut case, boys. We caught the man who seems to be the burglar."

Frank asked why the police suspected the man they had picked up.

Riley chuckled. "Well, we have some pretty good circumstantial evidence. Bill Adams saw the guy running away from Doc's house with a jimmy in his hand. We caught him going into the woods about a quarter of a mile away."

"And the money?" Joe asked.

Riley frowned as he turned a corner. "That's one thing that has us puzzled. We've looked for it everywhere. No luck!"

The car pulled up to the curb in front of a large, old-fashioned brownstone house. Frank and Joe hopped out, followed by Riley and Chet.

After climbing a flight of stone steps, they entered Dr. Gladstone's office. There they were greeted by Chief Collig, who got to the point quickly.

"We have the suspect in the next room. He'll be booked for possession of burglary tools. But he insists he didn't steal any money from Doc's house.

"My men have taken photographs of the jimmied window and cashbox. That's where all the money was." With his thumb he indicated a metal box on a table.

"Did anybody here touch anything in the room?" Frank asked.

"Only Dr. Gladstone. He used the phone to call us," Collig replied. "Otherwise, there hasn't been a soul in this room that we know of for a week, until Dr. Gladstone came in this morning after a seven-day illness. Whoever left prints on the table, the window, and the cashbox is the one who stole the money."

Joe said, "Okay, Chief, we'll get to work."

The Hardys picked up their fingerprint kit and started from the room, calling to Chet to join them. The boy looked puzzled. "Hey, what are you going outside for?"

Joe explained that trained criminal investigators learned long ago that the best way to find latent prints is by trying to put themselves in the burglar's place, mentally and physically.

"We're pretty sure the thief entered the office by the window," Joe said. "We'll check the outside of the sill, the panes, and the ledge for latent prints."

Frank and Joe found that the window was not far aboveground. They squinted at the glass from various angles in order to get a clearer view. Chet looked, too, and suddenly exclaimed, "I see a print!" He pointed to a darkish spot.

Frank shook his head. "That's only a smudge, Chet." He explained that a smudge is a smear of a print with no identifiable ridge pattern.

"Oh," said Chet, disappointed. He was about to touch the window when Frank warned, "Stop! You're violating the cardinal rule of preserving evidence. Many times people accidentally spoil latent fingerprints in this way."

"Sorry," Chet said.

Frank studied the window carefully, then said excitedly, "There are lots of prints along the bottom of the sash and the sill. And here are some beauties on the glass. I'll dust first, then we'll photograph them before lifting them."

"That's what I want to see!" Chet said.

"Well, watch me here," Frank suggested. He pointed to a portion of the window about midway in the frame.

"On glass, which is not backed up by any colored object on the other side," he said, "we can use either the gray or the black powder for our lift. But before we take a picture, we must back up the print by white paper if we use black powder, or black paper if we use gray powder."

Frank dusted the prints with gray powder. Then, while Officer Riley held a large black backup card inside the window, he photographed the first print.

Chet craned closer to watch. He noticed that Officer Riley had scotch-taped a small slip of paper in one corner of the backup card bearing Frank's initials, the date, and the numeral One. Before Frank took the next shot, Riley changed it to numeral Two.

"Why is he numbering the pictures?" Chet asked Frank.

"Because the investigator has to make notes about the crime scene processing and on all evidence located so that it can be properly presented in court," Frank explained. "Sometimes evidence is collected which can never be used in court, simply because it was not put together properly or was not maintained correctly. In some cases, a police officer cannot testify effectively due to incomplete notes."

"I see. In other words, you have to be very systematic."

"Right. Now let's lift the fingerprints."

Joe trimmed a piece about one and a half inches square from the sheet of rubber tape and removed the plastic covering from the sticky side. He handed the tape to Frank, who applied it over the first latent print.

"You see, Chet," he said, "I put one end of the tape down and roll the rest across the print. This way I get a nice smooth lift."

He peeled the tape off carefully and replaced the

transparent plastic covering over it. Then he initialed, dated, and numbered the back of the tape, just as Riley had done with the photographs, before going to work on the next print.

When all the latent prints were lifted, the Hardys gathered up their equipment and Frank said, "We'll go inside now."

They went to the physician's office to search for more latent prints. Three were discovered on the side of the window frame.

Their next job was the desk. "The cashbox was in the right-hand drawer," Chief Collig told them.

"Chet, try your luck and see what you can find," Frank suggested.

"Me?"

"Sure. Why not?"

Chet beamed Frank's flashlight obliquely on the surface of the desk. Suddenly he yelled triumphantly, "Here are a whole bunch of prints!"

Chief Collig and the Hardys came closer and took turns peering through the magnifying glass at the maze of patterns.

"Sorry, Chet," Frank said quietly, "but they're all smudges except this one." He placed a white chalk ring around the one he had pointed out. Seeing how crestfallen Chet was, he added, "Go ahead, dust it."

Chet selected the grayish powder for contrast and dusted it on lightly. Slowly the ridges appeared. He stepped back and gazed admiringly at his handiwork.

"Now take the camera," Frank told him. "I've already focused it and set the lens opening and shutter speed for the film we're using. Put the end of the adapter trough firmly on the desk, and don't forget to number your pictures."

Frank watched while Chet followed his instructions. "Perfect," he said. "Next you trip the shutter without moving the camera. Always remember to take two or three shots and to advance the film after each exposure."

When Chet had finished photographing the print, Frank asked him to lift it.

Chet selected the black tape to contrast against the gray powder and did as he was told.

"Good work," Chief Collig commented. "Now tackle the table and the cashbox."

Frank and Joe flashed their lights on the table and looked disappointed. "Nothing but smudges," Joe murmured.

"Right," Frank agreed. "Well, let's try the cashbox."

They scrutinized the small green metal container on the table, its lid jimmied open. Several papers were strewn nearby.

At that moment Chet looked up to see an elderly, bespectacled man enter the office. "Fellows, here's Dr. Gladstone," he announced.

"How are you, Doctor?" Frank said, recognizing the physician. "Too bad about this. Were these papers in the cashbox?"

"Yes," Dr. Gladstone said sadly. "That's all the burglar left."

Joe spoke up. "Were you the one who discovered

the theft, and has there been anyone else in the room today?"

"Well, I was coming down the stairs when I heard a noise. I opened the door with my key and noticed that the side window was open. It was then that I saw the rifled box on the table and called the police. I didn't touch anything else in the room except the phone."

The doctor turned to speak to the chief. Meanwhile, the Hardys located several good prints on the cashbox, which they dusted, photographed and lifted.

"Now what?" Chet queried.

"We'll take prints of the suspect. Okay, Chief?" Frank said. "Bring the kit, Joe."

At a nod from Collig everyone went into the waiting room. A dejected-looking small man with furtive eyes sat on an old-fashioned straight-back chair, guarded by a husky policeman.

The suspect watched worriedly as Joe set down the small black box the boys had brought along. They called this the Hardy Fingerprint Recording Kit. It contained a tube of printer's black ink, a small rectangular piece of clear plate glass, a rubber roller, a metal fingerprint card holder, a jar of gasoline, some paper towels and a number of FBI standard fingerprint cards.

Frank placed a few daubs of the ink on the plate-glass slab and with the roller spread it over the surface.

Noticing that Chet was watching intently, he said, "We roll the ink just enough so we can get a smooth coat on the fingertips. A good way to know if we have too much or too little is to hold the glass up to the light. When there's a light-brown film it's okay."

Meanwhile, Joe got out the FBI standard fingerprint cards. Chief Collig began asking the suspect questions in order to fill in the required data.

When the man gave his name as Jed Silvers, the police chief advised him of his constitutional rights to consult a lawyer before making any statements. Then the chief said, "You're from Redmont, aren't you?"

"Yes."

"Didn't you get out of jail only last week?"

"Yes."

Turning to Frank, Chief Collig said, "He's a petty larceny crook who is always in and out of jail."

While the chief continued to fill out the card, Joe said to Chet, "Take a look at this. The standard FBI card has spaces for the two types of impressions involved in fingerprinting. In the upper ten spaces the prints of each finger are taken separately. These are known as rolled impressions. At the bottom of the card, prints of the four fingers of each hand are taken at the same time; then the two thumbs are printed together. These prints are called plain impressions."

Joe picked up the card that Chief Collig had completed and clamped it firmly to the desk with the metal holder from the kit to prevent it from slipping.

Then he asked Silvers to clean his hands with gasoline by rubbing them together. "For the cleaning job," he said to Chet, "you can also use alcohol, or benzene—whatever you have available."

"Didn't you get out of jail only last week?"
the chief asked

Joe gave Silvers a paper towel to dry his hands. Standing at the man's right side, he took Silvers' right hand and inked the thumb from the tip to below the first joint by rolling it lightly from right to left on the inking plate. Then he rolled it on the fingerprint card in the same direction.

"You roll each finger only once," he explained to Chet, "and you print the fingers separately, beginning with the right thumb and then index, middle, ring, and little finger."

As Joe proceeded, Chet noticed that contrary to the thumb, the fingers were rolled from the left to their right side, or away from the suspect's body.

"Do you think you could do the same with his other hand?" Joe asked Chet.

"I'd like to try."

"Here again, the thumb is rolled toward his body, but the fingers are rolled away from his body."

"Do I stand on his left side or his right?"

"Whichever you prefer."

Chet accomplished his job with a proud grin.

"Great work, pal," Frank said. "Now, in order to complete this card, we'll record Silvers' plain impressions."

The four fingers of the right hand were inked, then pressed simultaneously on the space designated. When the left hand was completed, both thumbs were inked and printed together.

"Why do you need both rolled and plain impressions?" Chet asked.

"Rolled impressions are better because the pattern

area is usually completely visible. The technician whose job it is to classify the prints uses the plain impressions as a check on the sequence of the rolled impressions. In other words, it is positive proof that the proper fingers were put in the correct spaces."

Chief Collig interrupted. "Look, boys. We must make five complete sets of cards for the various law-enforcement agencies. Let's get going!"

They rapidly completed the task. Then the Hardys compared Silvers' fingerprints with the latent prints they had found. Surprise registered on their faces.

Finally Joe blurted, "Chief, the prints on the window and the sill are identical with Silvers'. But unless I'm mistaken, the ones on the desk and the cashbox belong to somebody else!"

"What?" Collig declared in amazement.

"I told you I didn't take the money!" Silvers shouted. "But you wouldn't believe me!"

"Maybe you didn't take the money, but you sure jimmied the window," Joe said. "You didn't have time to steal anything, because you were scared off when Dr. Gladstone came down here. Isn't that the truth?"

Silvers hung his head in silent confession.

Just then Frank recalled a family scandal involving the doctor's nephew. On a hunch he asked, "Dr. Gladstone, was your nephew Don here recently?"

"Yes," the doctor replied haltingly. "He wanted money but I ordered him from the house. It was the night I got ill. I don't like to talk about it, because you know the disgrace he caused my brother when he was involved in that car theft. You don't believe that Don—" The man's voice trailed off with the sad realization that his nephew was a prime suspect.

"Let's go over to headquarters and check these prints against Don Gladstone's in our file," said Chief Collig. He added, "Silvers, you'll be properly charged and held for the court."

The whole group went to headquarters and Collig requested that the card with Don Gladstone's prints be brought to his office immediately. They compared the impressions on the card with the lifted prints from the cashbox. They were identical!

"This clinches the case!" Frank exclaimed. "Don Gladstone stole the money, not Silvers."

The doctor, saddened by the results, nevertheless congratulated the Hardys. Chief Collig thanked them, saying, "When your father returns tomorrow he'll be surprised to find the case solved. You boys did a real professional job."

Frank and Joe grinned with pride, and Chet beamed. "I never thought I could learn fingerprinting so quickly. When's our next case, fellows?"

FOR MORE DETAILS ON FINGERPRINTING
TURN TO CHAPTER XII, PAGE 197.

CHAPTER III

THE CASE OF THE SHABBY SHOES

Shoe Prints, Tire Marks, Plaster Casts

IT was late Sunday morning. Frank and Joe were sitting on the front porch of their home with Tony Prito, a high school friend.

When Mr. Hardy appeared in the doorway, Tony said, "Hello, Mr. Hardy. Frank and Joe were just telling me about reproductions of shoe prints."

"That's right," Mr. Hardy replied, pulling up a chair. "As a matter of fact, we can do the same with tire marks or any other impression in sand, mud, dirt, and even snow. This is called positive identification."

Joe spoke up. "When we helped Dad on one of his cases, he showed us how to make reproductions of shoe and tire prints with plaster of Paris; also how to take impressions of tool marks. This is called moulage."

Mr. Hardy chuckled. "The most famous example of moulage identification," he said, "was the case where a burglar took a bite from a piece of cheese and the bite impression positively identified him as the criminal."

"I'll be careful hereafter where I eat cheese," Tony commented with a grin.

"Say, Dad," Frank remarked, "how about teaching Tony something about positive identification?"

"Certainly. We'll make a detective out of him yet."

"What's this all about?" Tony asked. "Something dangerous? If so, count me in."

"You'll see," Joe said.

Frank went inside and returned with a box. "This is the Hardy Plaster Cast Kit," he told Tony. "It contains two half-gallon cans with lids. In one can there's plaster of Paris. The other is empty. In addition, the kit has a number of flexible metal slats from a Venetian blind, a wooden stick, some clothespins, and a can of clear plastic spray."

Tony looked at the contents of the kit with considerable curiosity. He said, "I know you mix plaster of Paris with water and pour it to make a mold, but what are these other things for?"

"A metal slat," Frank explained, "is used to enclose the molding mixture in whatever size is needed. The clothespins hold the ends of the slat together. The plastic spray is needed to firm up dust, sand, or snow before the plaster of Paris is poured in. It also retards the heat effect on the snow when the plaster is setting. And the wooden stick is for stirring the plaster mix in the can."

Mr. Hardy said, "How would you like to go on a case with us, Tony? Chief Collig is going to pick us up soon."

"That would be great, Mr. Hardy. Thanks!"

"You're welcome." The detective continued and his tone grew serious, "Mr. John Nelson, a wealthy Bayport businessman, was struck on the head near the driveway of his home. It appears that he was robbed. He's in the hospital, unconscious."

"How come they're calling us in on it?" Joe asked.

"Well, as you know, the chief is sort of short-handed right now. Several of his men are not available for various reasons, so he asked me to do him a favor and help him out."

Mr. Hardy stood up and began pacing around the porch. "The chief phoned me that there are footprints in the shrubbery beds and tire marks on a dirt road running along the side of Mr. Nelson's property."

Just then a police sedan pulled up and Chief Collig stepped out, his gold badge and braid shining brightly in the morning sunlight.

Seeing Tony, he smiled. "Fenton, have you added another assistant to your detective team?"

"Could be," Mr. Hardy replied jovially as everybody entered the sedan. Frank carried the kit.

A few minutes later the uniformed police chauffeur pulled up in the driveway of a large home.

"This way," the chief directed. "The shoe prints are

over here. I had Officer Williams protect the crime scene."

Mr. Hardy approached the spot carefully, with his young assistants close behind. He scrutinized the impressions from various angles, then said, "The ground is soft and there are quite a few shoe prints, two different lengths. It appears that there were two men hiding in the shrubbery."

He beckoned the boys to come closer. "See these cigarette stubs? One's pretty long, the other one's been smoked all the way down to the filter. They'll be collected as evidence."

Mr. Hardy turned to Chief Collig. "Did your people take photographs of the crime scene yet?"

The chief nodded. "They're being developed in the lab right now."

Frank spoke to Tony. "When pictures are taken, it is essential to include the photographer's initials, the date, and a ruler in every shot."

"Why a ruler?" Tony asked.

"By comparing the object you photograph with the ruler, you can ascertain its actual size," Frank replied.

"How about getting to work on the casts, boys?" Mr. Hardy asked. He pointed to the shoe prints.

"Sure, Dad," Frank said. He and Joe began to mix the powder with water, which Tony had got from a nearby spigot.

"The mixture should be stirred constantly until it has the consistency of melted ice cream," Joe explained.

Mr. Hardy said, "Notice how I've placed a metal slat around this shoe print, Tony? I've put mud and stones on the outside of the slat, so that when we pour the mixture, it will not move.

"Okay, Joe, pour the stuff in." As Joe did so, his father went on, "In order not to spoil the print, we pour the plaster on a piece of glass or a flat stick and let it drip gently into the impression. When it's about three-fourths of an inch thick, we reinforce the plaster by placing sticks on the surface."

"Why?" Tony wanted to know.

"So the cast will not break while it is being handled."

Joe added another three-fourths of an inch of the wet plaster. "Now we've got to wait twenty to thirty minutes before we remove the cast," he said. "See how easy it is?"

"Why, anybody could do it," Tony replied.

"That's right," Mr. Hardy agreed. "But the more one practices, the better one becomes at it." He pointed to other shoe prints. "Boys, make casts of these four here," he said. "Tony, suppose you practice on this one." He indicated one print apart from the others. "Meanwhile I'll look at the tire marks with the chief."

The two men walked away and Joe mixed another batch of plaster. Frank used more metal slats and made borders around each print. Then he checked the first cast which was beginning to harden. He smoothed out the surface with a piece of glass.

"What are you doing that for?" Tony asked.

"To give it a professional touch. Also, it makes it easier for the investigator to mark his initials, the date,

How to Make Plaster Casts

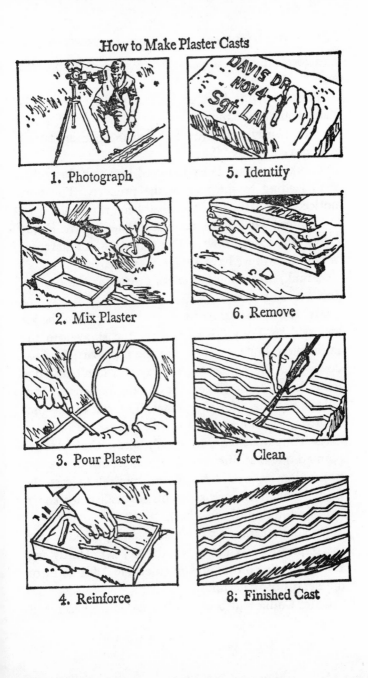

1. Photograph

5. Identify

2. Mix Plaster

6. Remove

3. Pour Plaster

7 Clean

4. Reinforce

8. Finished Cast

and location with a pocketknife or a sharp-pointed stick."

Tony had just finished his cast when Officer Williams approached them.

"Mr. Hardy wants you to bring the plaster-cast kit to him right away," he said.

Frank, Joe, and Tony followed him to a dusty dirt road leading to the rear of the property. The boys noticed that part of the road had been roped off.

"I hope we'll have enough plaster," Mr. Hardy called out to the boys. "These impressions here are very good and we have a large area to cover.

"Frank, find some flat sticks to use for the border. Joe, get some water."

Mr. Hardy took the can of clear plastic from the kit and said to Tony, "Never direct the spray into the impression, but over it so that the mist particles float down into the pattern. This way you don't dislodge loose dirt or dust. When the plastic hardens, it provides a firm base for the plaster. The rest of the procedure is the same as for the shoe prints."

As Tony watched Mr. Hardy spray, the detective pointed out that due to the greater length of the tire impression, it would be more practical to cast the print in eighteen-inch segments for a distance covering one rotation of the wheel.

Joe finished mixing the plaster and poured it into the impression. While it was drying, Mr. Hardy suggested, "Let's go over to the chief. He'll fill us in on the details of the crime."

Chief Collig had been conferring with Officer Williams, and now turned to Mr. Hardy, "Fenton, here's the story," he said. "Last night, about ten o'clock, Mr. Nelson drove his car into the garage after returning from a business conference."

"Wait a minute," Frank put in. "Yesterday was Saturday. Isn't that unusual?"

"Well, Mrs. Nelson told me that her husband has met people before on weekends, especially if they're from out of town. She had just opened the front door to greet him last night when she heard him call for help. As she ran down the walk, Mr. Nelson staggered and fell, crying out that he had been robbed.

"Mrs. Nelson noticed the sounds of running footsteps and a short time later the starting of a motor and the noise of a car as it roared down this roadway. She saw it turn onto the main road and head toward town.

"She tried to help her husband. But he was unconscious and blood was streaming from a scalp wound. So she immediately called the First Aid Squad. In her shocked state she did not think of phoning the police. When the squad reached the scene, they rendered first aid, took Mr. Nelson to the hospital, and notified us. Dr. Robinson said that if they hadn't stopped the flow of blood when they did, Mr. Nelson would not be alive now."

The chief paused briefly, then continued, "Two of my men went to the hospital to question Mr. Nelson. They were told he was unconscious and might be for a long time. Dr. Robinson's diagnosis was that the man had been struck with a blunt instrument on the head and right arm, and that he was suffering from a possible skull fracture and fracture of the upper right arm.

"Then they went to Mr. Nelson's house and spoke to his wife. She told them what had happened. They searched the area with floodlights and found the shoe prints and tire marks. They also discovered a baseball bat with bloodstains on it near the front walk. Mrs. Nelson identified it as belonging to her nephew. The boy was here a couple of weeks ago."

"Where's that bat now?" Mr. Hardy asked.

"Officer Rinshaw processed it for fingerprints but there were none. He thinks they were rubbed off with a cloth or handkerchief."

"He's probably right," Mr. Hardy said. "Now let's see. We know that Mr. Nelson was robbed. Of how much, we must find out. We know that at least two persons ambushed him.

"They must be familiar with this area, because they knew where to park their car so the victim would not see it. We can be reasonably sure that one of them, at least, is a professional criminal because he left no fingerprints on the bat. We also know what kind of cigarettes they smoked."

"Correct, Fenton," said Chief Collig. "One brand is Zara, an unusual cigarette of Turkish tobacco. The person who smokes that brand threw the butt away after it was only half-consumed. The other brand is a common one. This person smoked it clear to the filter."

Frank, Joe, and Tony went to check the tire plaster

casts. When the segments were dry, they removed them from the retaining slats and brushed off the soil adhering to the casts with a soft paintbrush.

"You have to be careful not to scratch a cast or alter any detail when cleaning it," Frank explained to Tony. "Don't ever use hard or sharp instruments or wash the dust off with water."

Then the boys brought the casts to Mr. Hardy. He was pleased with the results. He said to Tony, "We can tell the make of the tire by the pattern. The FBI keeps a file of every brand.

"Now look at this. See where pieces of the tread have broken off, and note these scars. It's going to be easy to make a positive identification."

The boys hurried to get the casts they had made of the shoe prints.

"These are as good as any I've ever seen," Mr. Hardy said. "Take this larger print, for example. It was made by a comparatively new shoe, with an O'Sullivan heel. The two cuts in the rubber will easily identify the owner."

Next Mr. Hardy examined one of the other casts. It was apparently that of an older, half-soled shoe. The rubber heel, Cat's Paw brand, was well worn, especially on the outside rear edge.

"The man who wears this shoe," Frank observed, "walks splay-footed."

Later, everyone involved in the investigation held a conference at police headquarters. Chief Collig assigned various officers to specific tasks. Mr. Hardy asked his sons and Tony to call on all sellers of tobacco in town to inquire whether they stocked Zara cigarettes, and if so, who their customers were.

The boys' survey revealed that only four dealers sold Zaras. From the proprietors they got the names of the persons who regularly purchased the brand. They were reputable citizens, except one!

Mr. Pogatch, who owned the town's leading tobacco shop, told the boys that for the past week a stranger had been buying Zaras. The man, about forty years old, was six feet tall, slender, and distinguished looking. He wore rimless glasses, was well-dressed, and spoke with a Midwestern accent. From a remark the customer had made, Mr. Pogatch assumed that he was staying at the Bayport Hotel. Zaras were not sold there.

The three young detectives went immediately to the Bayport Hotel and talked with Alec Small, the desk clerk, whom they knew well. They repeated Mr. Pogatch's description of the Zara customer. Mr. Small informed them that the man was Andrew Sissler from Indianapolis.

"He registered together with a man from New York named Arthur Booth," the clerk added.

"What does Booth look like?" Frank inquired.

"He's about thirty years old, five-feet six-inches tall, and slender. He has a prominent, long, thin nose, sharp-pointed chin, and unusually large ears."

The clerk looked at Frank and Joe speculatively. "Working on a case with your father?"

"That's right," Joe replied with a grin.

"What case?"

"We're not at liberty to say," Frank replied, knowing that a good detective should never tip his hand.

Alec Small nodded. "You don't have to tell me anything. But I've got a hunch it's the Nelson case. I heard Mr. Nelson got robbed last night."

"News travels fast," Joe said.

Mr. Small grinned. "My sister's a nurse in the hospital." He paused for a second, then went on, "I have certain suspicions and I feel that as a citizen I should communicate them to the proper authorities."

"Suppose you tell us," Joe said.

"No. Not because you're boys, mind you, but because the information is so important. I want to talk to Chief Collig, or your father."

"We'll get them," Joe declared, and the three hurried back to headquarters.

Mr. Hardy and Chief Collig, meanwhile, had visited Bayport Hospital. Mr. Nelson had regained consciousness but was presently sleeping and could not be disturbed. He had told Dr. Robinson that he was attacked by two men, who grabbed his briefcase containing ten thousand dollars, most of it in large denominations.

As Mr. Hardy and the chief stepped from the front entrance of the hospital, a patrol car carrying Frank, Joe, and Tony came to a halt at the curb. Joe quickly relayed their findings.

"Good work," the chief said. "Let's go see Alec Small."

Before they drove off, Mr. Hardy instructed his sons and Tony to question people around town about Booth and Sissler. "We'll meet in an hour at the hotel. Good luck, boys."

When the detective and Chief Collig confronted the

clerk, Mr. Small beckoned them into his office and closed the door.

"Over a week ago," he began, "Sissler and Booth registered here. Sissler did most of the talking. He claimed they were businessmen seeking a site for a manufacturing corporation in Bayport."

"What were your suspicions?" Mr. Hardy asked.

"Well, for one thing they didn't act like business people. They slept late and loafed around the hotel a lot. But in the evening they always went out."

The clerk took a deep breath. "About eight o'clock last night, I saw Mr. Nelson in the lobby. He was carrying a brown-leather briefcase, and asked what room Mr. Sissler was in. I told him, and he went upstairs. Half an hour later he came down again. I know him quite well, so he stopped and we talked a while. He mentioned something about going to Center City. Then he left. That's the last I saw of him."

"Then what happened?" Chief Collig asked.

"Right after he left, Sissler buzzed me to get him a telephone number, which I did. I recognized it because I had gotten it for him several times before. I made a note of it each time because I have to add the charges to his bill."

Mr. Small reached into his desk drawer. "Here it is."

"Hm!" Collig said. "A local number. I'll find out from the telephone company to whom it belongs. What happened next, Alec?"

"About eleven last night, Mr. Booth walked in. He appeared rather nervous as he asked for his room key. Then he hurried upstairs."

Alec Small looked at his wristwatch. "At one o'clock, just about two hours ago, Sissler and Booth came downstairs. Sissler was not in his usually jovial mood. As a matter of fact, he seemed uptight. He asked me to make up bills for both of them; they were checking out. I did and they left. Now, gentlemen, I don't know if these facts mean anything to you, but they sure seem suspicious to me."

Mr. Hardy said, "Alec, you're absolutely right. Thanks for telling us."

He turned to the chief. "How about searching the rooms these men occupied?"

"Good," Collig said. Before they followed Alec Small upstairs, he called the telephone company and the supervisor promised to phone back with the information about the number Sissler had called.

Then they searched Sissler's room on the second floor but found nothing of importance. "I'll send someone over to look for fingerprints," Collig said. "Alec, make sure nobody cleans this room until then."

Booth's room across the hall was scrutinized next. In the corner of a closet Mr. Hardy found a pair of shabby shoes with traces of mud. As the detective examined the soles and heels, he gave a low whistle. "Ezra, did you bring a set of those photographs your man developed of the shoe prints taken at the Nelson house?"

"Right here," Collig said and pulled them out of his pocket. The men looked at them closely.

"There's no doubt that Booth was one of the assailants," Mr. Hardy declared. "These are the half-soled shoes with Cat's Paw rubber heels that left the impressions we found at the scene of the crime!"

Chief Collig scraped the soil off the shoes into a large envelope, then sealed it and marked the outside for identification.

"I'll forward this and soil samples from the area where we located the prints to the FBI laboratory," he said. "If they're found to be identical in makeup, we'll have some more constructive evidence."

The three returned to Mr. Small's office with the telltale shoes. Just then the telephone rang. The clerk answered and handed the instrument to Collig. "It's about that number," he said.

The chief jotted down a few notes, thanked the caller, and hung up.

"Fenton, it's the Shady Rest Guest House on the outskirts of Bayport. I wonder what the connection is."

"We'll soon know," answered the detective. "I think we'd better—"

At that moment the door flew open and Mr. Hardy's three assistants rushed in.

"Hey, Dad, do we have news!" Joe said. "We asked around as you suggested. When we talked to Jimmy Watkins, the shoeshine boy, he told us that he'd seen Sissler and Booth in a car belonging to the Portside Auto Rental Agency. A big man was with them."

Frank took up the story. "So we went to the Portside Agency. We spoke to the manager. He told us Booth and Sissler had been renting the same car, a current model black sedan, for the past few days. They took it out again yesterday morning, and Booth did not bring it back until after ten-thirty last night."

Tony exclaimed, "And, Mr. Hardy, there was mud

"These shoes left impressions at the scene of the crime,"
Mr. Hardy said

on the tires! We were told that Sissler and Booth showed up this morning and are still out in the same car."

"Maybe they're at the guest house," Mr. Hardy said and told the boys about the phone number that Sissler had called several times.

"I know the place," Tony said. "It's off the main highway on the road to Griggstown."

The chief outlined his plan. "I'll send a radio car to Griggstown and have it head back toward the guest house. I will approach Shady Rest from the direction of Bayport and the place will be in between our two cars. If those men try to escape, we'll get them either way. And we'll keep in radio contact with each other at all times."

Collig dispatched a car with three police officers and allowed it a head start to coordinate the movement. After some debate, he agreed to take the Hardy boys and Tony along with him, under the condition that they stay in the background to avoid danger.

"After all, we want to see the finish of this case," Joe murmured to his brother.

With the chief's chauffeur at the wheel, the sedan sped quickly toward the Shady Rest Guest House. The other driver had been instructed to keep watch from a hill overlooking the house and to report any activity.

A metallic voice crackled over the police radio. "W2MAX calling. Three men just left the guest house. One is carrying a suitcase, the other two large bags. They seem to be in a hurry. Got into a black sedan and are coming your way. What do you want us to do?"

"Follow and stay behind them. If they try to turn, head them off. We'll set up a roadblock on the narrow part of the highway just before the bend."

Upon reaching the bend, Collig's driver quickly swung the car across the road, making it impossible for anyone to pass. The boys were ordered into the woods in case of gunfire.

Frank, Joe, and Tony had hardly hidden behind the trees when they heard the roar of an approaching motor. The chief and his chauffeur, with drawn guns, were crouched behind their car, one at each end.

The suspects' vehicle came in sight around the sharp bend, kicking up a cloud of dust. The squeal of brakes filled the air as the careening car nearly struck the side of the chief's sedan.

As the driver frantically manipulated the wheel the two passengers in the rear seat were thrown violently backward. The driver backed up, turned, and raced off.

"They're getting away!" Joe shouted.

Just then the car veered to the right and crashed against a large oak tree. Despite the shattering impact, the driver jumped out and started for the woods, an automatic pistol in his hand.

By this time the other police car had reached the scene. Chief Collig and two officers started after the fleeing man. "Halt!" yelled the chief and fired two shots into the air.

The man turned to look at his pursuers and did not see the broken tree limb ahead. He tripped and fell, striking his head.

The police officers pounced on him and in a moment he was handcuffed. The automatic was picked up from the ground. Chief Collig, meanwhile, seized the other suspects, sprawled dazedly in the car. They were quickly handcuffed, searched, and advised of their rights.

As soon as they had recovered from the shock, the larger of the two demanded to be set free. The chief, who had recognized him as Sissler from the tobacco shop owner's description, silenced him quickly.

"If I were you, Sissler, I'd keep my mouth shut. Mr. Nelson is very ill at the hospital. If he dies, you may have to face a murder charge."

By now the boys had emerged from cover and approached the wrecked car. Frank looked at its tire prints in the soft earth. He bent down to study them, then shouted excitedly, "Chief, this is the car that was at the crime scene!"

As Frank and Tony crowded around him, Chief Collig pulled several photographs from his pocket and Frank pointed to the identical patterns and scar marks.

Joe and a police officer came forward with the men's luggage and a large manila envelope. The chief opened the latter and took out a tied stack of negotiable bonds.

The luggage contained only personal articles and clothing. "Let's put all this stuff into my car and take it to headquarters," Chief Collig said.

The three fugitives were herded into the squad car and one of the policemen took the rental car back to Bayport.

At headquarters the three men were fingerprinted.

"Halt!" yelled the chief

The Identification Division of the FBI was contacted. Identification of Sissler and Booth was confirmed. The third man, August Findal, was described in an FBI Wanted flier as a fugitive from justice. He was wanted along with John Scudder, alias Arthur Booth, for the daylight holdup of a bank messenger on a New York City street three weeks earlier. The negotiable bonds in the manila envelope were identified as belonging to the bank.

The prisoners were then questioned by Chief Collig separately. Sissler and Booth had waived their rights, but Findal refused to make any statement, even after being confronted with the FBI flier and the bonds.

Sissler, who admitted being an ex-convict specializing in confidence games, did not need much prompting. Chief Collig's statement that Mr. Nelson might die had scared him and he made a full confession. Frequently, however, he interspersed his statements with protestations of innocence regarding the assault on the merchant.

Sissler, a man of numerous aliases, had been released from prison a month before and needed money desperately. Three days after the New York holdup, he was approached by Booth, whom he had met in prison. Booth asked Sissler if he would undertake to sell the negotiable bonds. His cut would be one-third. Sissler readily consented.

He and Booth came to Bayport, where they met Findal. The latter had been hiding out at the guest house. Findal convinced them that Bayport would be an easy town in which to sell the bonds. He had heard stories of Mr. Nelson, who was somewhat eccentric and kept large amounts of cash in his own safe at home.

The three made their plans with Mr. Nelson as the target.

Sissler approached the merchant on Saturday and offered to sell him the bonds for a discount since he needed cash before the weekend was over. He told Nelson that he had been threatened by loan sharks from whom he had borrowed money and they insisted on repayment before Sunday night, and that he feared for his life unless he could meet the demands.

Finally, he thought he had hooked his fish and planned to close the deal the preceding night. Nelson had called at the hotel and told Sissler that he had the money with him but that he had changed his mind about concluding the transaction. He mentioned that he was going to Center City to confer with a friend who owned an investment firm and would call Sissler later.

After Nelson had left, Sissler telephoned Booth and Findal at the guest house to tell them what had happened. Findal was furious, blaming Sissler for not closing the deal right away.

Sissler insisted that he did not know his two partners had robbed Mr. Nelson until shortly before they were apprehended.

Booth was questioned next and repeatedly denied everything. But after being confronted with Sissler's statement, his own shoes, and the casts of their imprints at the crime scene, he began to show signs of weakness. When he was told that the car he had rented had been positively identified by a comparison of its treads and the impressions left at the scene, he confessed.

The prisoner stated that he was induced by Findal to go to the merchant's house. The original plan was for Findal to hold up Mr. Nelson with his gun. The victim was to be bound and gagged with adhesive tape and dropped off in the woods. Booth declared that he was shocked when his partner used the bat he had found at the scene. Findal had explained his action by saying he did not want to waste any time and that he did not hit Mr. Nelson hard.

The mystery now seemed to revolve around the whereabouts of Mr. Nelson's briefcase and the money. The three prisoners did not have the loot with them, nor was it found in Findal's suitcase or the bags of the other men.

Chief Collig dispatched two men to the guest house to see if they could locate it. They returned shortly with only a lock, similar to those found on expensive briefcases, but now blackened. The officers reported that the owner of the Shady Rest had told them Findal had burned some personal belongings in his incinerator. A search among the ashes had revealed the lock.

Frank examined Findal's suitcase closely. Suddenly he uttered an exclamation, felt around the bottom, and pulled up a heavy lining. There was the missing ten thousand dollars!

Later in the day, Chief Collig and Mr. Hardy visited Mr. Nelson at Bayport Hospital. He assured them that he felt better and insisted upon hearing the details of the case. He said that he had not suspected

Andrew Sissler of any wrongdoing and had delayed closing the deal only because of his habitual caution.

"I went to see a friend in Center City who is in the investment business and asked for his advice regarding the bonds," he said. "And since my friend had no unfavorable information, I planned to pay Sissler the money!"

At dinner that evening at the Hardy home, where Chief Collig and Tony had joined them, Joe said, "Chief, what about the clue of the Zara cigarettes? We know that Sissler smoked them. A butt was found at the scene of the attack and still Sissler says he wasn't there!"

Chief Collig laughed. "He happened to leave a pack in the car. When Findal was at the Nelson house, he ran out of cigarettes and smoked a Zara. It was one of those lucky breaks which happen occasionally in investigations. The cigarette clue was a very important lead!"

Tony observed, "The positive identification offered by the plaster casts was great. Even if there had been no other evidence, I think it would have been strong enough to convince any jury. And the most amazing thing is that almost any boy can learn to be an expert at it!"

CHAPTER IV

THE SAFECRACKER'S CALLING CARD

Identifying and Capturing the Fugitive

THE steady patter of rain echoed monotonously in the large factory. Cyrus Cook, the night watchman, trudged wearily through the maze of storerooms with a small time clock on his shoulder.

He muttered to himself as he walked along. "Now I can rest for fifteen minutes."

Cyrus slumped into a battered old chair, removed his shoes, and rubbed the soles of his tired feet.

The watchman was in his early sixties, and he had worked thirty years for the Ajax Watch and Jewelry Company in the small town of York. His duties were light but dreary. Forty-five minutes out of each hour he spent punching his time clock at nine locations in the building. He wished the night were over.

Suddenly Cyrus heard a suspicious noise above the steady drumming of raindrops. He rose from his chair and shuffled through the warehouse, shining his flashlight left and right. As he neared a darkened storeroom, the light fell on three hooded men!

Cyrus froze in his tracks for an instant, then turned to run for the telephone. The men lunged at him. The watchman was blackjacked, tied in a heavy wooden chair, gagged, and blindfolded.

When Cyrus Cook regained consciousness, he could hear the sound of metal against metal not far from him and knew the company's safe was being cracked. As he sat helpless and frustrated, he pondered how the hooded men had managed to get into the plant without setting off the burglar alarm.

After what seemed an eternity, the safecrackers retreated, their footsteps echoing down the corridor.

"I must do something!" the watchman thought.

He wriggled the chair along the floor until he reached a wall. Then he bounced himself to a desk with a telephone. His fingers fumbled with the dial, but finally he managed to get the operator. He called for help in a muffled voice.

Minutes later there was loud banging on the outside door, then the burglar alarm went off. The lights were turned on, and Cyrus saw two policemen who took off his blindfold and hastily untied him.

The first thing the watchman did was to shut off the burglar alarm. Next he looked at the ripped safe and telephoned Mr. Herbert Taylor, president of the Ajax Watch and Jewelry Company.

The police, meanwhile, had discovered a ladder propped against the skylight in a rear room. They questioned the watchman about it. Cyrus said the ladder belonged to Ajax, but had not been there earlier, and the skylight had been ingeniously disconnected from the alarm system. Apparently the ladder had been used by the burglars.

Mr. Taylor, a brisk man with a black mustache, arrived at the plant at four A.M. He stared at the safe in shocked disbelief. Then he turned to the watchman and angrily demanded to know what had happened.

After Cyrus related his experience, Mr. Taylor's attitude softened. "I'm glad you weren't hurt," he said.

Then he went to the telephone and dialed. His face brightened as he said, "Is that you, Fenton? . . . This is Herb Taylor. Could you please come to our plant immediately? My company's safe has been burglarized. The thieves stole ten thousand dollars in negotiable bonds, fifteen thousand dollars in gold and silver used in jewelry manufacturing, three thousand dollars in cash and some new and invaluable jewelry designs."

There was a slight pause, and Taylor continued, "I'm sorry if you were about to take your boys and their friend on a vacation trip. Could you postpone it? . . . Bring them along and I'll see that they have a vacation in my summer home."

Another slight pause, then Mr. Taylor went on, "I'm ever so grateful, Fenton. . . . What do you mean by protect the crime scene? . . . Yes, the police are here. I'm sure they're taking care of it. You'll arrive in about four hours? . . . Fine. Good by."

One of the policemen asked, "Were you talking to Fenton Hardy? If he's coming, I'm sure the chief will be glad to work with him. He's practically a genius in his line."

"Yes, he is," Taylor replied. "I'm not so worried about the cash and the bonds, but the designs cannot be replaced. That's why I'd like to have him in on this."

A little after eight o'clock Fenton Hardy, his sons Frank and Joe, and their pal Chet Morton arrived at the Ajax factory. Mr. Taylor greeted his old friend warmly, and Mr. Hardy introduced the boys.

Then he said, "Herb, I'll need to know all the details. But first I want to see the mode of entry and then examine the safe."

Mr. Taylor took him to the rear room of the building where the ladder still stood under the skylight.

"Go to it, Frank," Mr. Hardy ordered.

Frank climbed the ladder and noted that two large panes of reinforced glass had been removed from the skylight. Putting his head through the opening, Frank saw that a long rope, knotted approximately every foot, was lying on the roof. One end was tied to the chimney.

Frank correctly surmised that after the panes had been taken out, the safecrackers had tied one end to the chimney and lowered the other end into the building. That was how they had entered.

The boy examined the metal frames of the skylight with his magnifying glass. He took a long pair of tweezers from his pocket and removed some lint and fibers and some whitish material from the frame. Then he placed these in separate envelopes on which

Two panes had been removed from the skylight

he noted the contents, source, his initials, and the date.

After he had descended with the clues, his father went to the safe. He took a close look at it and the tools which had been left next to it. Then he said, "Seems as if Moose Wetzel did this job."

Chet nudged Joe and whispered, "How does he know who did it?"

"Dad remembers Wetzel's manner of working from a case years back. Also, he quickly scanned his Modus Operandi file on safe burglars before we left this morning."

"Modus Operandi?" Chet asked.

"It's a technique perfected by law-enforcement people to help combat crime. Modus Operandi is a Latin expression meaning method of operation."

"I see," Chet said.

"Through the years," Joe went on, "the police have discovered that criminals use distinct techniques when committing crimes. Take a house burglar, for instance. There are a lot of ways to break into a house. The burglar might pick the lock of a door, jimmy a window on the first floor, or break the glass in the basement. Usually he will enter a house the same way every time."

Frank added, "There are other factors involved in the Modus Operandi." He jotted them down for Chet while the detective examined the safe.

Scene	Associates
Entry	Vehicle
How entered	Victim
Time of day	Odd and unusual acts
Loot	Alias or nickname

Frank handed his friend the piece of paper and said, "Under *scene,* you put the kind of building, store, automobile, or whatever else represents the scene of the crime. You generally find that a house burglar rarely breaks into a store. Whatever he specializes in, he will stick to and seldom changes.

"Under *entry,* you put the manner of entry. Under *how entered,* you insert the use of specific tools, ladder, aided by accomplice, and any other factors.

"*Time of day* is vital because a criminal will operate nearly always at a specific time."

Joe took up the explanation. "*Loot* is also important. For example, certain house burglars will take only cash and nothing else. Others may include jewelry.

"Some specialize in furs. In recent years some steal only credit cards or blank checks and personal identification papers. Those are sold to others who fill out the checks, forge them, and use the identification to cash them.

"Under *associates* you state whether one or more persons took part in the criminal act and what each one did.

"*Vehicles* are studied to determine if a car was used in a crime and if it was stolen.

"Under *victim* you write the sex, age, and background of the person assaulted. For example, some muggers will only attack elderly people, others only young women.

"The item *odd and unusual acts* is extremely important. Often a criminal will leave the same characteristic clue. For instance, one might cut a pane of glass in a sort of circle. Another criminal might make a diamond-shaped cut or add his own personal flourish to the job. It's like planting his calling card at the scene of the crime.

"*Alias or nickname* is often important in identifying the criminal."

"I understand," said Chet.

"You forgot to mention one important thing, Joe," Frank put in, "the criminal's photographs in the Modus Operandi file, if any are available."

Fenton Hardy, meanwhile, had been taking photographs of the crime scene. Then he drew a sketch and Frank and Joe helped him by taking the measurements of the room.

Mr. Hardy explained to Mr. Taylor that through

his study of safecrackers he knew there were seven ways to open a safe.

"The one used most today is the Rip Job," he said. "An electric drill and a sectional jimmy—which is nothing more than an extremely large can opener—are used.

"The second method is the Punch Job. Sledge hammers and a chisel are used to knock off the dial and punch in certain pins. Then there is the Chopping Job. A sledge, chisels, and sectional jimmies are generally used on the bottom of the safe. The fourth method is the Drag, or Old Man Job. This, however, is practically obsolete now. Drills were used to break the spindle around the dial.

"The Blow Job was also employed a great deal in the past. Nitroglycerine was placed in holes drilled in the safe and other recesses. Then it was detonated. The sixth way is the Torch Job, also seldom used today due to the danger of detection. An acetylene torch, or a burning rod, is used to burn a hole in the safe.

"The last method," Mr. Hardy went on, "is known as the Jimmy Valentine. The safe is opened by manipulating the combination. These are mostly inside jobs, meaning the criminal has wormed himself into the company as an employee or has access in some other official capacity. Or he finds the combination somewhere, in a desk drawer perhaps, or on the back of a calendar."

The detective added that when he had entered Mr. Taylor's office he had noted by the condition of the safe and by the tools left at the scene that it was a

Rip Job. This immediately narrowed the number of suspects who might have committed the crime.

"When I found that the skylight had been used, it was just as if Moose and his pals had signed a confession."

Mr. Hardy said that Moose Wetzel, who always changed his associates with each job, was probably the only one in the area who entered buildings through skylights. He always bought new tools in some distant city and left them at the crime scene. Also, he ripped open the safe by cutting across the door diagonally.

Then the detective directed his sons to dust everything for latent fingerprints. "I'm sure you won't find any, because these men are professional criminals and wear gloves," he said to Chet. "However, we never take a chance of missing any possibility, so we go through the process of searching a crime scene according to regular patterns."

While looking for prints, Joe noticed a brown windbreaker lying on the back of a chair in the office. It was wet.

"This was evidently left by one of the burglars," he told Chet.

He examined the windbreaker carefully, looking and feeling in every pocket.

"What can you prove with it?" Chet asked.

"I'm not sure yet," Frank replied. "There's nothing in the pockets, but here is a dry-cleaner's mark. Most State Police laboratories maintain a file of laundry and dry-cleaner's marks."

"That's true," Mr. Hardy said. "The State Police

here have one of the best in the country. This windbreaker is a vital clue in identifying the criminal. We'll take it to the State Police today."

Mr. Hardy led the three boys toward the ladder. "Do you notice anything unusual on the floor?" he asked.

"There are some shoe prints!" Chet volunteered.

"Good. If they can be clearly seen, they're good evidence."

Frank took out his flashlight and shone it obliquely over the tile floor, making the details more visible. They searched for the best prints. When they had located two, Frank marked them with a piece of white chalk.

By this time Joe had taken a camera and a large piece of lifting tape from their kit. He laid a ruler close to the shoe prints for purposes of comparison, and also a piece of paper with his initials and the date. Then he set up the camera so that the lens was directly over the prints. He took several pictures.

"Are you going to lift the prints just as you did with the latent fingerprints?" Chet asked.

"Right," Joe said. When he had completed his task, he showed the lifts to the others. They were exceptionally good, finely detailed. They were heel marks of the right shoe, bearing the peculiar design of a five-pointed star. On it was a ragged gash apparently caused when the wearer of the shoe stepped on a piece of glass or sharp metal.

Mr. Hardy nodded approvingly. "Boys, this is a fine piece of evidence." He turned to Mr. Taylor. "We can find out the make and size of the shoe. The

FBI lab maintains a shoe-print file of all rubber and composition heels, half soles, and whole soles manufactured in this country."

The detective went on to say that the photographs would be permanent records of these clues.

"We'll make several copies and distribute them," he said. "The heel print is so unusual that I'm sure we'll have no trouble in making a positive identification when we obtain the shoe of the suspect."

"A thief stands no chance at all with investigators like you!" Chet exclaimed with admiration.

A search of the outside of the building revealed that the criminals had climbed up to the roof by means of an extension ladder. It was discovered that it was the property of a painter who had left it alongside a nearby house.

The Hardys and Chet now went to police headquarters. Here a copy of the description, photographs, and fingerprints of Moose Wetzel were obtained from Chief Logan. As the group looked at the pictures, a policeman standing nearby exclaimed, "I saw that guy at the Center Luncheonette yesterday! He was having coffee and talking to the waitress. I'm sure it was the same guy because of his bulbous nose. I'd know him anywhere."

"Wetzel was probably casing the factory and making plans," Mr. Hardy said. "Let's go talk to the waitress."

On the way to the car Chet asked curiously, "Do you think she can tell us much?"

"You never know," Joe replied. "One of the best ways to get information is by interviewing people."

"Right," Mr. Hardy said as they approached the Center Luncheonette. "For example, bellboys, bootblacks, waitresses, taxi drivers, postmen, salesclerks, and storekeepers can be a good source of information if they had any contact with the suspect."

He added, "Many investigators develop a contact file. On an index card they write the name, address, and description of people they think might be helpful. They add to this card all they know about the person. Then, whenever they have an investigation in the section of the town where the person lives or works, they have a valuable contact."

"You should see Dad's contact file," Joe said. "He has thousands of names in it."

Mr. Hardy, Chief Logan, and the boys interviewed the waitress at the luncheonette. She remembered talking to the man described and identified his photograph.

According to her, Wetzel asked a lot of questions concerning the town. He was well dressed and gave the impression that he wished to go into business in York. He inquired about the Ajax company and the police force.

On the basis of this and the Modus Operandi data, Logan went to the local court, made a complaint against Wetzel and obtained two John Doe warrants for Wetzel's associates.

Joe explained to Chet that a warrant is a court order for the arrest of a suspect. When the criminal is not known, the warrant is made out for the arrest of "John Doe."

Mr. Hardy then asked Chief Logan to issue a tele-type alarm to all police in nearby states.

"When the Wanted Notice is forwarded to the FBI in Washington, that agency, too, will look for the offender," he said to Chet.

"It will be only a matter of time," Chief Logan declared, "before we get him."

"That's true," said Mr. Hardy. "But we want him now before he sells all the loot!"

Chet studied a copy of the teletype alarm. "This is quite a long description, isn't it?" he asked.

"No," answered Frank. "This is what we call the short form of the Portrait Parle."

Chet looked puzzled, and Joe explained. "Portrait Parle is important in criminal investigation. It's a French term, meaning speaking likeness. French scientists contended in the early half of the nineteenth century that no two human beings were alike."

Mr. Hardy supplied the following information: In 1870 a French anthropologist, Alphonse Bertillion, devised a system to measure the dimensions of certain bones in the body and to record them. From these a composite formula could be derived which, theoretically, would apply to only one person. The system was based on the theory that the pertinent measurements would not change during an adult's life.

A thorough description of the subject arrested was made along with the measurements. This method was used for about thirty years. However, it was prone to inaccuracies as it required special training on the part of the persons making the measurements, and the equipment used to make them was expensive. Also, there were cases when an identification could not be made merely upon the basis of the measurements formula. Therefore the system was discontinued about 1903 and followed by the use of fingerprint identification.

"Outstanding peculiarities, like a wart on somebody's nose, or a limp, are important in identifying a suspect and would be noted," Mr. Hardy concluded. "And this is what a Portrait Parle looks like." He showed a couple of forms to Chet.

PORTRAIT PARLE

Short Form

Name _____

Aliases _____

Sex _____

Race _____

Date of Birth _____

Place of Birth _____

Height _____

Weight _____

Build _____

Hair _____

Style _____

Eyes _____

Glasses _____

Complexion _____

Scars or Marks _____

Tattoos _____

Peculiarities _____

Armed or Dangerous _____

Long Form

Name _____
Aliases _____
Sex _____
Race _____
Date of Birth _____
Place of Birth _____
Height _____
Weight _____
Build _____
Hair _____
Color _____
Style _____
Beard _____
Mustache _____
Sideburns _____
Eyes _____
Glasses _____
Ears _____
Nose _____
Mouth _____
Chin _____
Complexion _____
Scars or Marks _____
Tattoos _____
How Dressed _____
Occupation _____
Social Security Number _____
Residence Address _____
Marital Status _____
Wife's Name _____

STANDARD DESCRIPTION OF PERSON

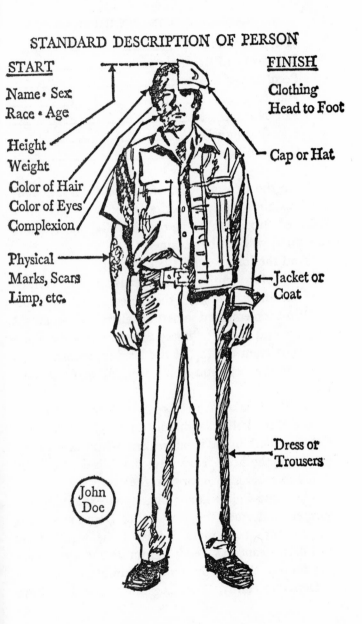

START

Name · Sex
Race · Age

Height
Weight
Color of Hair
Color of Eyes
Complexion

Physical
Marks, Scars
Limp, etc.

FINISH

Clothing
Head to Foot

Cap or Hat

Jacket or
Coat

Dress or
Trousers

John
Doe

Wife's Residence _____
Relatives and Residences _____
Peculiarities _____
Habits _____
FBI No. _____
F.P. Classification _____
Criminal Record _____

"The short form," Mr. Hardy said, "is generally used to give a brief description of a subject for a 'Wanted Broadcast.' Some of the individual features, of course, will not be obtained."

"And the long form?" Chet asked.

"That's for identification bureaus and for 'Wanted Notices,' and is used when the subject is interrogated."

"I just remembered something else that Dad taught us," Joe said to Chet. "Every time you describe a person, start from the top of the head and work downward. In that way you won't overlook or forget anything."

Mr. Hardy asked Chief Logan to dispatch an officer to the State Police laboratory to check on the drycleaner's mark in the windbreaker. Meanwhile, photographs of the heel prints were developed and distributed to everyone working on the case.

The State Police laboratory, upon examining the garment, informed the York Police Department that the cleaner's code mark indicated the windbreaker had been cleaned at Teddy's Laundry and Dry Cleaning Shop in the nearby city of Columbia.

Detective Hardy, Chief Logan, and the boys drove

there to interview the owner. Theodore Katz revealed that the windbreaker belonged to Ernest Wetzel, who had been a customer for about a year. He owned expensive clothes, mostly of the sports type.

Katz said that Ernest was a quiet fellow who always had come in alone, except about a week ago when he had been accompanied by a stranger. He had introduced him as his brother.

"Do you remember what this man looked like?" Mr. Hardy asked.

"Oh yes. I could never forget his face. He had a big nose that was shaped like a light bulb!"

"Do you know Ernest Wetzel's address?" Chief Logan queried.

"He lives on Poplar Street. I can't remember the number, but it's the last house next to Clark's Ice Cream Parlor."

After thanking the dry cleaner, the group went to Columbia Police Headquarters. Here they conferred with Sergeant Clooey, in charge of the Detective Bureau. The sergeant said that Ernest Wetzel was indeed the brother of Moose. There was another brother named Horatio.

Ernest and Horatio lived together on Poplar Street. Clooey added that as far as he knew, they were law-abiding citizens.

"On the basis of our evidence," Mr. Hardy said, "I'm afraid you'll have to arrest them."

It was decided, however, not to make any arrests unless the brothers could be apprehended at the same time.

The Wetzel house, a small Colonial with a screened-in porch, was immediately placed under surveillance by the local police, including Sergeant Clooey, Chief Logan, Fenton Hardy, and the boys.

Chief Logan said, "I wish one of us could get into that house under some pretext and find out if they are there."

Chet spoke up. "I'll go! I can pretend to sell magazine subscriptions!"

"Great idea," Frank agreed.

"If you should get hurt, I'd have a lot of explaining to do," Sergeant Clooey said thoughtfully.

"I'll be all right," Chet declared. "Why should they bother me? I'm only selling magazines."

Fenton Hardy backed Chet's idea. The husky boy had often helped his sons on their cases and could handle almost any situation.

"There's a stationery store down the block," Joe said. "We'll go and get an order pad and a pen, so you'll look authentic."

A short time later they were back and Chet began to "sell magazine subscriptions." He started at the beginning of the block and worked his way toward the Wetzel house. When he finally reached it, hidden policemen had their eyes on him. The Hardys waited tensely as Chet rapped on the door and entered the porch.

"I hope he's all right," Joe whispered to Frank from his hiding place behind some bushes.

Two minutes passed. Then Chet emerged, whistling. He walked slowly to the next corner, turned, and hopped into a waiting police car. All the investigators gathered immediately.

"What happened, Chet?" Mr. Hardy asked.

The boy took a deep breath. "The door to the porch was open. I walked in, and the door to the house was also open a little bit. I heard one man say he wanted to see a movie at the Tivoli. Then another man answered, 'Okay.' The first man said for him to get ready, because the main feature would start in twenty minutes."

"Look! They're leaving!" Clooey called. He had been stationed at the corner to watch the house.

A car was backing out of the driveway. The entire group scattered behind the buildings. The prowl car backed into an alley. As soon as the Wetzels had driven away, everyone gathered again.

"They definitely are the Wetzels. I recognized them," Sergeant Clooey said.

"Good," Mr. Hardy replied. "Suppose you plant two men in the theater to spot them. When they leave, your people will be right behind them. We'll make the arrest when they come out of the place."

The sergeant nodded. "Let's go."

Everything went as planned. When the Wetzels walked out of the theater, Mr. Hardy and Sergeant Clooey snapped handcuffs on their wrists. The prisoners were hustled into a police car after being advised of their constitutional rights.

"Incidentally, Chet," Joe said mischievously as they drove back to headquarters in another squad car, "did you sell anyone a subscription?"

"Thank goodness, no!"

At headquarters the Wetzels were searched. No clue of value was uncovered, and they indignantly protested their innocence. But when Ernest was told that he had forgotten his windbreaker at the scene of crime, Horatio cursed his brother.

"I knew that would get us into trouble, you stupid idiot!"

After this, it was easy to extract a statement from the brothers, who refused the assistance of a lawyer. They admitted burglarizing the Ajax company with the help of Moose, who had planned the job. They denied they had the money, bonds, precious metal, or the designs and insisted that Moose had gone off with everything.

They claimed they did not know where he was, and executed a voluntary waiver of search for the house and grounds, which meant they agreed to a search of the premises by the police.

The loot was not found. On the way out the rear door, Frank spotted a trash can near the side of the house. He walked over to it and deliberately scattered the contents on the walk.

"What are you doing that for?" Chet Morton asked.

"Trash cans frequently are good sources of information," Joe explained, while Frank poked among the debris with a stick.

"I don't see any clues," Joe remarked, glancing at a conglomeration of empty cans, old newspapers, and a crushed milk carton.

"Wait a second," Frank said and picked up the

milk carton. Using his pocketknife, he cut off the top. *Inside were tiny bits of torn white paper!*

Frank whistled. "This is a note and here are two of the words: 'loot' and 'lie low'!"

"It might be the key clue," Sergeant Clooey said, a note of excitement in his voice. "Let's piece it together at headquarters."

Minutes later Frank and Joe were working over a jigsaw puzzle of paper bits at a table in the Detective Bureau. Using plastic tape, they patiently fitted piece after piece together. Finally they were finished.

"Wow!" Frank exclaimed as he read the note. "Listen to this, Dad!

" 'Dear Ernie and Horatio,

I think it's best to lie low for a while, so I'm leaving for Clinton right now. When I feel the coast is clear, I'll come up with the loot and whack it up. It's better if I'm not seen with you now. Be careful and keep your mouths shut.

Moose' "

"Well," said Mr. Hardy, "that note proves that Moose has the loot."

"And it tells us where he is!" Frank said elatedly.

"You still don't have his street address," Chet put in.

Mr. Hardy said there were many possibilities to explore. These included the Clinton telephone directory, city directory, friends and relatives, the gas and electric company, credit bureaus and collection agencies, the post office, finance companies, and voting registration lists.

"But our best bet," he concluded, "is the Motor Vehicle Bureau."

A telephone call quickly produced the information that Daniel (Moose's real first name as shown in the police records) Wetzel was listed as the owner of a new Oldsmobile; also that he lived at 373 Rutherford Street in Clinton.

"Boy, the trap is closing!" Chet exulted. "Let's go get him!"

"We'll have to ask the Clinton police to make the arrest," Frank told his pal. "Police can't act outside their jurisdiction unless they're actually chasing a suspect, but out-of-town officers who are familiar with a case often work with local authorities."

"You mean if a policeman is in another town and he sees somebody kill a person, he can't do anything?" Chet asked with indignation.

Joe laughed. "Of course he can. Anyone can make a citizen's arrest when he actually sees a felony committed."

Fenton Hardy was already on the phone talking to Deputy Chief Hansen in Clinton, whom he knew well. He asked Hansen to produce a search warrant for Wetzel's home. The officer assured Mr. Hardy he would have it ready by the time they arrived in Clinton and would accompany them to the Rutherford Street address.

Chief Logan, Mr. Hardy, and the boys immediately departed for the nearby town in the chief's car.

From Clinton Police Headquarters, Hansen led the way in his car, accompanied by a plainclothesman.

The address turned out to be a bungalow on a dead-end street next to a wooded area. No one was home, but the back door was unlocked.

Deputy Chief Hansen, Chief Logan, and the Clinton policeman began to search the house. Mr. Hardy beckoned the boys into the driveway. "I think Wetzel left in a hurry," he said. "Otherwise he would have locked the back door. Also, he did not take his car. There's a chance he kept the loot in it. Let's check out the garage."

Joe was first to enter. "The keys are in the ignition!" he called out. "Wetzel must have been about to take off when he saw us coming. He probably left on foot."

Frank and Joe searched the inside of the car, while Mr. Hardy opened the trunk. In it he found a metal box. "This might be it, boys!" he said. "Frank, get the officers. Joe, see if you can force the lock on this with a tire tool."

When Frank returned with the others, Joe had succeeded in opening the box. "Money!" he cried. "And the bonds are here, too!"

Further search of the trunk revealed two canvas bags of gold and silver scraps and a manila envelope with jewelry designs.

"This is the loot from the Ajax company," Mr. Hardy told the officers.

"Money!" Joe cried

"Let's see if we can find any clue as to where Wetzel may have gone," said Frank. He, Joe, and Chet started to circle the house.

Suddenly Joe stopped short and stared at the ground.

"What's the matter?" asked Chet.

"A heel print with the star impression!"

"Here's another," cried Frank, who was scanning the ground farther on. "They seem to go into the woods!"

Caught up in the excitement of the chase, the boys followed Wetzel's trail among the trees.

"He was running here," Joe said.

"He was tiring going up this hill," Frank remarked after several minutes.

"How do you know all that?" Chet asked.

"Tell you later," Frank promised.

Finally the boys ran into rocky terrain where the trail seemed to stop. They stuck a stick into the ground next to the last print and covered it with a handkerchief. Then they began to travel systematically in a circle.

"Over here," Frank called.

The trail led straight to a cave, with its entrance half hidden by brush.

The boys retreated to a spot behind a rock which gave them a view of the cave.

"I'm sure Wetzel is holed up in there," Frank said in a low voice. "Joe, run back and bring Dad and the police. I'll stay here with Chet and keep watch."

After Joe had gone, Chet said, "That was great the way you followed the trail. How'd you do it?"

"We call it tracking," Frank replied. "First you study the print you are following. Figure out when it was made. If it has water in it, recall when it rained last. If it contains sand or grass seed, think of the last time the wind blew.

"Then you track against the sun. This way the impression casts a shadow which brings out the details better. But don't just look at the tracks. Lift your head once in a while and survey the criminal's trail as a whole. You might spot cigarette butts on either side of the track, matchsticks, loose thread, or other important clues.

"When tracking early in the morning, the earth and grass may be dewy. It's easy then because the marks are more visible."

Frank paused a minute and the two listened. Everything was quiet. Then Frank went on.

"It's hard to follow tracks on hard or rocky ground. You might have to go by small signs such as broken moss, cracked branches or twigs, upturned stones and leaves, which you will recognize by their moist and darker undersides."

"What do you do if you lose the trail?" Chet asked.

"Don't go wandering around before you mark the last track. You do this by inserting a stick in the ground and placing a handkerchief on it. Then see if you can locate the new trail."

"Pretty neat," Chet said. "Tell me more."

"You can deduce a great deal from studying tracks. For example, whether a man was running, walking slowly, or walking normally. You can figure out if he's carrying a heavy weight or if he has a limp. You can also ascertain whether he's trying to run into hiding."

"How?"

"A person who's running away to hide will turn around from time to time to see if he's being pursued. Then a few of his steps will point to either side and not in the general direction of the trail.

"We knew when Moose was running because the deepest part of the track was in the toe mark and the prints were wide apart. When he was getting tired, his steps were shorter and the toes were pointing outward. Also, the prints were deeper."

"What else can be learned from tracks?" Chet asked.

"Well, if a person's walking slowly, there will be short spaces between the prints with the emphasis on the heels. If he's walking normally, there's no emphasis on the heels. If he's carrying anything heavy, the prints are much deeper at the heels. If he has a limp, the marks show unusual or odd patterns."

At this point the two boys saw the rest of their group arriving with Joe in the lead.

"Get behind the rock with Frank and Chet," Mr. Hardy ordered Joe. "Wetzel may be armed and dangerous."

The officers all drew their guns and approached the cave. But Wetzel was in no mood to put up a fight. He knew he was trapped and came out with his hands over his head.

"Wow!" Chet exclaimed. As they walked back along the trail, he added, "Detectives sure have to know a lot."

CHAPTER V

THE SECRET OF THE EMPTY PAGE

The Powers of Observation and Memory

FENTON HARDY rose to his feet after examining the prone figure of a policeman on the roadway. "This is terrible," he said. "He's been shot to death!"

The detective turned to Frank and Joe and their pal Chet Morton. "Joe, jump in my car and call Chief Collig."

The crime scene area was a lonely stretch of the winding old road along a creek between Bayport and Center City. Mr. Hardy and the three boys were on their way for an afternoon of fishing when they had come upon the victim. No one else was in sight.

The policeman was lying face down in the center of the road, his head in the direction of Bayport. His crash helmet had fallen off and rolled a short distance away. A notebook and pen were in the dust near the body. The officer's right hand was extended over his head, still clutching his revolver.

His motorcycle was parked on the right side of the road approaching Bayport. The engine was running.

As was his usual custom, Mr. Hardy took notes and made a rough sketch of the scene. Joe returned and told his father that Chief Collig was on his way.

Within minutes a screaming chorus of police sirens could be heard. Three cars roared to a halt. Almost before they stopped, the chief was out on the road. He hurried over to the body and stared at it in shocked disbelief. Then he said in a choked voice, "That's my nephew, Tom Collig. Joined the department a few weeks ago. How can I tell his wife and three kids that he's dead!"

He turned to the elder Hardy. "What happened?"

"I don't know, Chief," Mr. Hardy said softly, "but it appears that he was shot twice in the back."

Collig nodded grimly.

"Ezra," Mr. Hardy added, "I want you to know how sorry I am. I'll do anything to help."

"Thank you, Fenton. I'll never rest until I catch the murderer!"

Meanwhile, Officer Higgins took photographs of the crime scene from several angles. As he did, the Bayport First Aid Squad arrived, followed by the city ambulance. A white-coated intern examined the victim and officially pronounced Tom Collig dead. The body was put into the ambulance.

Mr. Hardy and the police officers made a thorough search of the crime scene. They scoured both sides of the road for a considerable distance, with negative results. The roadway itself yielded no clues either.

While the men were busily engaged, Frank and Joe decided to walk along the road toward Center City. Chet followed them. After passing a sharp bend, he asked, "Why are you walking all the way up here?"

"Because you never know where you'll find a clue," Frank replied.

"But there is nothing! Let's go back," Chet said.

At that moment Frank and Joe stopped dead in their tracks. "Chet," Joe asked, "do you mean to tell me that you don't see anything unusual?"

Chet looked about and shrugged. "Are you kidding? There's nothing but a few pieces of glass near that pole."

Joe pointed to the left. "Not only are there a few pieces of glass, but if you look a little higher, you'll notice a scrape mark on the pole. That could mean a car speeding from Center City sideswiped it."

"So?" Chet asked.

"If you come closer to the pole," Joe continued, "you can see what appears to be dark-blue paint scrapes where it was struck."

"You're right! How come you notice all these things?"

"We've been trained by Dad to observe," Frank replied. "The power of observation, Chet, is based on our five senses: sight, hearing, smell, touch, and taste. The two that we use most are sight and hearing. It's a known fact that modern man does not use his five senses to their full capacity."

"As a matter of fact," Joe put in, "Dad says that people walk around completely oblivious to many things they see. Let me give you a concrete example." He took Chet by the shoulders and turned him about. "You've been with us all morning," he said. "What color shirt do I have on?"

Chet scratched his head. "I'll have to take a guess. Blue?"

Chet turned to face Joe. The shirt was green with white stripes.

"Oh, oh, I goofed!"

Joe continued. "There are a couple of good tests to show you how dormant your capability to observe may be. You pass the intersection of Main and Linden streets every day. Tonight, before you go to bed, picture what it looks like and write down these impressions. Tomorrow when you go there, you'll be surprised at how much you missed and how many incorrect impressions you have listed."

Joe turned to Frank. "I think you'd better get Dad and Chief Collig to look at this pole. It may be a clue. I'll tell Chet some more about observation."

As Frank sprinted down the road, Joe went on, "Chet, when you have some time, sit down and write as full a description as you can of some of your friends, teachers, and acquaintances. Keep the descriptions in your pocket. When you meet these people, compare your notes with what you see. You'll be amazed how inaccurate your descriptions are."

"Well, isn't there a way to improve one's power of observation?" Chet asked.

"Sure. But it takes a lot of practice!"

"I'd like to," Chet said. "But how?"

"Observation is nothing more than a series of mental images to which you apply the laws of repetition, association, attraction or its opposite, repulsion. Here, I'll give you some examples. If I were to ask you to draw a map of France, you probably couldn't, because you've never truly observed it. But I'll bet you could do a fair job on Italy. Why? Because the picture of a boot comes to mind. That's the association. If I ask you what seven times seven is, you'd give me the correct answer immediately because you have repeated this over and over. This is repetition.

"So it is with things you like. They strike your attention, leaving a permanent image. The same applies to things you violently dislike. Such as last year's math teacher."

"Wow! Could I describe him!"

"Another way to improve your powers of observation," Joe went on, "is to look briefly at any shop-window display. Turn around and write down what you saw. Compare it with the real thing and note the items you left out. Keep practicing until you become proficient. This is the way policemen train themselves."

Just then Frank came running back. "They'll be here in a minute," he said. Nodding toward Chet, he added, "Joe, did you tell him about memory?"

"No, I didn't yet. Just got through with observation."

"I'll do it, then," Frank volunteered. "Chet, memory works through association. We can recall a new idea only by connecting it to something we already know. We form these associations consciously and subconsciously. This can be improved by training."

At that moment Mr. Hardy, Chief Collig, and his men arrived. "What do you make of this?" the chief asked, pointing to the broken glass and the pole.

Fenton Hardy bent down and examined the splinters through a hand magnifier. Then he carefully looked at the pole.

"The broken glass seems to be from the headlight of a car," he said finally. "It's very fresh, so are the paint scrapings."

"How do you know the glass hasn't been here long?" Chet asked.

"It's simple. This road is very dusty. Whenever a car drives by, a cloud of dust rises. But there's no trace of it on these fragments."

Joe interrupted excitedly, "Dad, this means that since the time the car hit the pole, no one else has driven past here. So the last car we passed coming from Center City must have been the one that struck the pole and may have something to do with Tom Collig's murder."

"I remember the car," Frank cut in. "We passed it only a couple of minutes before we found the body. It was going very fast. A dark-blue sedan. Recent model."

"And it had a broken right headlight and a dented right fender!" Joe said. "There were three men in it."

"Correct," his father said. "I saw it, too."

"Not me," Chet said. "I just remember the car speeding by."

"Come to think of it, Dad," said Joe, "I looked at the license plate. It was covered with dirt, but the borders were yellow and it was the same size as the registration plates in our state."

At once Chief Collig radioed headquarters to set up roadblocks on all highways leading out of Bayport. He also notified police in the adjoining towns to be on the lookout for the car.

Higgins took photographs of the pole and the glass. Then the pieces were meticulously picked up. Using a sharp knife, Mr. Hardy cut away the paint scrapings which he placed in an envelope.

"What are you doing that for?" Chet asked.

"If we're fortunate enough to find the headlight from which the glass came, we'll fit the broken pieces together like a jigsaw puzzle. It will be positive proof that these pieces came from the damaged headlight.

"The scrapings and chips of paint will be sent to the FBI laboratory in Washington, D.C., to determine its exact composition. If we find the vehicle that scraped the pole, its paint can be compared with that on the pole to see if they're identical."

As the group slowly walked back to the waiting cars, Chet lagged behind, scanning the roadside. Suddenly he bent over and called out excitedly, "Come here quick! I think I've discovered something."

The others hurried to his side and Chet pointed among the weeds. There lay two .45 caliber shells, about three feet apart.

"Good work, Chet!" Frank said.

Collig called for Higgins to make close-up photographs, and Mr. Hardy included the position of the shells in his sketch.

"They probably came from an automatic pistol," Joe said to Chet. "You see, every time a pistol fires, its firing pin hits the primer at the base of the shell. This causes the explosion which forces out the lead bullet. The extractor hits the side of the casing and ejects the shell from the gun automatically."

Chet was impressed by his friend's knowledge of firearms.

"When the firing pin hits the center of the primer," Joe went on, "it leaves a distinct mark. If you compare a shell found at a crime scene with another from the suspected gun and the marks are identical, you can positively state that this was the gun fired. It can also be proved by the ejector marks."

"Does this go for revolvers, too?" Chet asked.

"Yes, but with these differences. In the first place, a revolver does not eject any shells. After firing, the shell stays in the gun and must be removed manually. For this reason, no extractor marks are on the bullet. But there's a firing pin, so you can prove that two shells with matching pin impressions were fired by the same weapon."

"Why are firing pin marks different in different guns?" Chet wanted to know.

Frank answered. "When you look at any firing pin, extractor, or ejector under a microscope you'll find definite characteristics. No two are alike. Then you use a comparison microscope to study both the known shell and the suspected shell. If the marks on both are exactly alike, you have made a positive identification."

"I see," said Chet. "Is that a comparison microscope you've got in your lab?"

"Right."

"Hurry, boys," Mr. Hardy called. "We have a lot of work to do."

Chief Collig said to the detective, "I just radioed headquarters. There's no word on that sedan yet."

"Well," Mr. Hardy replied, "I think our next step is to check all the service stations in Bayport to see if the blue car was brought in to have a headlight repaired."

Several police officers, along with Frank, Joe, and Chet, were assigned to check the garages. The reports were negative. As the trio trudged back toward headquarters, Joe said, "Let's take a shortcut through the park."

"Okay," Chet agreed. "The soft grass will sure be easier on my poor tired feet." He grinned. Walking along a narrow lane in Bayport Park, Chet suddenly stumbled and pitched headlong to the side of the path.

He let out a whoop that startled Frank and Joe. "What's the matter, Chet? Did you hurt yourself?" Frank asked.

"No. But look!" Chet pointed to the shrubbery.

Frank and Joe parted the bushes and gasped. *There stood an empty blue sedan!*

Chet scrambled to his feet and they walked around it cautiously without disturbing anything. The right

There stood an empty blue sedan!

headlight was broken and the fender was smashed.

Joe could hardly believe their good luck. "How in the world did you see it, Chet?"

"When I fell, I noticed tire ruts on the grass. They seemed fresh. And they led to the car. I saw it through a crack in the foliage."

Frank slapped Chet on the back. "You're learning fast!" Then he added, "We'd better get to a phone pronto."

"I'll go," Joe offered. "You stay here to protect the evidence." He was one of the fastest men on the high school track team and disappeared like a shot.

Shortly two police cars with Fenton Hardy, Chief

Collig, and other members of his force arrived in the park and screeched to a halt.

An examination of the sedan revealed two bullet holes in the rear. The chief and Mr. Hardy noticed that attempts had been made to remove all fingerprints by rubbing the car's surface with a cloth.

However, they discovered a number of visible prints on the back of the rear-view mirror and a latent print on the rear window.

Higgins photographed and lifted them and rushed them to the fingerprint section for processing and identification. No other clues were found in the car and it was towed to the police parking lot, while everyone drove to headquarters.

Chief Collig contacted the Motor Vehicle Bureau. Within a few minutes a teletype came back. The car had just been reported stolen by its owner, who had left it in a parking lot in Center City.

"Obviously the criminals changed cars in Bayport," the chief said, and ordered that the roadblocks be continued, and also that train stations, the bus terminal, and the airport be kept under surveillance.

Then he said to Mr. Hardy, "Fenton, let's have another look at the sketch you made at the scene of the—"

A knock on the door interrupted him and Officer Riley walked into the office. "When the repairman came to fix our teletype machine, he found this message stuck in it. It had been sent from Center City at ten A.M., Chief," he said, and handed Collig a piece of paper.

The chief glanced over the message, then said, "Listen to this: 'The Center City Bank of Commerce was held up by three armed bandits this morning. One of them had a .45 caliber pistol. He ordered the cashier to fill a brown paper bag with bills. The robbers wore handkerchiefs over their faces and the man with the gun had a white piece of adhesive tape above his right eye. According to witnesses, the robbers escaped in a blue car!'"

"Dad," Joe cried out, "maybe it was the bank robbers who killed Tom Collig!"

"I'm sure there's some connection," Mr. Hardy said. He frowned. "Ezra, do you have Tom's report book here?"

"Sure." Chief Collig ordered one of his men to bring it in. Mr. Hardy opened the notebook.

One page had been torn out!

"Chief," the detective said softly, "your nephew wrote something on that missing page. Someone did not like it. After Tom turned his back, this person shot him, tore the page out, and threw the book on the road. Tom lived long enough to fire twice at the escaping car. That's the way I see it. Now what could he have written?"

"Probably information from the driver's license of that person," Collig replied. "Perhaps he was going to give him a summons!"

Mr. Hardy examined the book again. He noticed indentations on the blank page following the missing one, and squinted at it from various angles.

"I can make out the name and address," he said

slowly, "also the license number—Amos Chipman, 142 Parade Street, New York City, W8 113 47212 55343, or 848. And it goes on to say: age forty-two, five-feet eight-inches, one hundred and eighty pounds, adhesive patch above right eye!"

"Now we know for sure that the driver of the car was one of the robbers who held up the bank in Center City!" Frank exclaimed.

Chief Collig asked Officer Riley to telephone the New York police for information on Chipman.

Mr. Hardy said, "And I'll call the Center City police for fuller details on the holdup." He went into the office next to Collig's.

A few minutes later he returned and said the Center City police chief was sure that the blue car found in Bayport was the one used in the holdup. The driver had stopped for gasoline at a station on the outskirts of Center City. He seemed to be in a great hurry, refusing to let his windshield be cleaned. The attendant noticed the patch of adhesive over his right eye and remembered that he threw a Lozino panatela cigar wrapper to the pavement.

Just then Officer Riley finished his call to New York and reported that Amos Chipman had a long arrest record, beginning with larceny and including several holdups. He had been released from prison five months before and was wanted for violation of parole. Riley concluded by saying that all information, including rogues' gallery photographs, would be sent by special delivery and that Chief Collig should have them in the morning.

Bayport policemen, meanwhile, scoured the city

for the suspects. Next morning everyone involved in the case met at headquarters. Chief Collig was tired and red-eyed from lack of sleep. All talked in subdued voices.

"Have you checked the field interrogation reports yet?" Mr. Hardy asked him.

"Sure." Collig scowled unhappily. "There's nothing of importance."

"What are field interrogation reports?" Chet asked Joe.

The young sleuth explained that they were forms used by police in progressive communities on which officers jot down anything unusual they observe while on duty.

"For example," said Joe, "last year when the safe at Commonwealth Supermarket was cracked, the police could never have solved the case without an officer's field interrogation report. In this case the policeman observed a car parked in a lot near Commonwealth late at night. It didn't seem to belong there, so he noted its license number. From there on it was simple to break the case because it had been the burglar's car."

Chet said, "I wouldn't know what to include in these reports."

"It's a matter of judgment," Frank said. "For instance, a man crossing the street, tripping and grabbing his hip may have a gun. A kid driving an expensive car may be an auto thief, so might be a person moving from one parked car to another, or seen loitering near a car. A car traveling at high speed may be fleeing from a crime."

"I see," said Chet.

Joe picked up the interrogation forms and scanned them briefly. About midway through the pile he lifted one up and called to his father, "Dad, take a look at this! It says that Patrolman McDonald observed a stranger early yesterday morning walking slowly back and forth on the opposite side of the street from the Union Bus Terminal. He crossed the street twice, but did not go into the terminal. The officer talked to him briefly. He told McDonald that his name was Alonzo Chip, that he lived at 243 North Auglis Street, and that he was waiting for his brother to come in from Center City."

Officer McDonald's notes gave the description of Chip as about forty-two years old, five-feet eight-inches tall, about one hundred and eighty pounds. He smoked a long cigar and has a large mole over the right eye. McDonald concluded his report by stating that Chip walked south on Lyons Avenue and that was the last he saw of him.

"Might be something there," observed the chief. Then he asked Riley to bring McDonald to his office.

"Mac's been on the force only a year," he said to Mr. Hardy. "And he's very meticulous with his reports. Good man."

Meanwhile, the information on Chipman had arrived from New York and was handed to Chief Collig.

It contained fingerprint classification, a copy of Chipman's record, and photos. A complete description noted the following peculiarities: He frequented taverns, had a large mole over his right eye, repeatedly scratched his nose, and smoked Lozino panatela cigars.

Chief Collig ordered Higgins to compare the finger-prints found on the sedan with those forwarded from New York.

Then Officer McDonald was ushered in. When questioned about Chip, he confirmed the observations in his report and added that the man appeared nervous. He looked at the photographs from New York and studied them intently, but said he could not make a positive identification.

Collig praised the patrolman for his alertness and filing the field interrogation report, then McDonald left. He was hardly outside the door when Officer Higgins came in excitedly. "Without a doubt," he declared, "the fingerprints behind the mirror and on the rear window of the blue sedan belong to Amos Chipman!"

"Wow!" Chet exclaimed. "The case is solved!"

"Not quite," Joe stated. "We still have to catch Chipman, remember? Then the pistol must be found and identified as the gun used. And we must find out who fired it!"

"And," Frank added, "we have to recover the stolen money!"

Mr. Hardy held up the full face photo of Chipman. "Chief," he said, "please have copies of this photograph made and give one to every police officer. Since the Lyons Avenue section has a lot of rooming houses, I would concentrate manpower in civilian clothes to scour that area."

Collig nodded. "I was thinking along the same lines."

"Dad, what can we do?" Frank spoke up. "May we cover the Lyons section with the police?"

"No. I have a special job for you."

"What's that?"

"I want you to go into every store and eating place around Lyons Avenue and show the owner and employees the picture. The minute you locate someone who has seen Chipman, call me."

"Okay, Dad."

After the boys had obtained copies of Chipman's photograph, Frank and Joe examined it carefully.

"Why are you doing that?" Chet asked.

Frank replied, "Here's where we use our powers of observation again, this time to create a mental picture of the man. We imprint in our minds his prominent features or peculiarities: the sharp thin nose, the large mole over his right eye, his long head and deep-set eyes. When we hear the name Chipman from now on, we'll associate it with all this."

Chet nodded. "Let me see that photo for a minute." He, too, studied it, then the trio set off for the Lyons Avenue section. It was a community of older buildings. Chet and the Hardys went from one place to another, asking questions and showing the picture. But no one had seen Chipman.

They trudged in and out of stores, restaurants, diners, rooming houses and went through the age-old experience of professional detectives—wearying legwork.

Finally Frank remarked gloomily, "We're almost through and have gotten exactly nowhere."

The perspiring Chet sat down on the curb. "Don't you think we'd better go back?" he asked. "There are no clues around here!"

"Nothing doing," Joe said. "A good investigator never quits. We have seven more places to try."

At that moment he noticed Chet staring at something on the other side of the street. He turned and saw a man walk into the grocery store they had just left.

"That was Chipman!" Chet blurted. "He sure looks tough!"

"Are you sure?" Joe could hardly believe it.

"Positive!"

"Okay," said Frank. "I'll go in and see what he's up to. When he comes out, you two follow him."

"Okay," said Chet, and Joe nodded in agreement.

Frank crossed the street and entered the store. He stood a little to the rear of the man as if waiting for his turn. He was unable to see the suspect's face. The man was ordering a variety of cold cuts and canned goods from a prepared list he held in his hand.

The stranger's manner was that of any normal customer and Frank began to wonder if Chet had been mistaken. As the storekeeper was totaling the bill, the customer added, "I'll take a dozen Lozino panatela cigars, too."

The words electrified Frank and he stood rooted to the floor. His eyes fell on a suspicious bulge in the man's right rear hip pocket. Was it the death-dealing .45 caliber pistol?

The suspect paid with a twenty-dollar bill, took the

change, and turned. Frank got a good look at him. He was Chipman all right.

"What'll you have, son?" asked the shopkeeper.

Concealing his excitement, Frank said in a calm voice, "A pound of sugar, please."

As soon as Chipman had walked out, the storekeeper said, "Wasn't that the man whose picture you showed me?"

"It was. And thanks for not giving me away. May I use your phone to call Chief Collig?"

"Sure, go right ahead." The man pointed to the wall phone and Frank gave the police chief the information.

"Be careful," Chief Collig cautioned. "This guy is a killer. If something happens to you boys, your father will never forgive me. I'll alert all unmarked police cars. They'll be there in one minute. Your dad and I in two!" He hung up.

Frank hurried from the store to catch up with Joe and Chet, who were following Chipman. The robber was walking at a rapid pace, and the two boys were a good distance ahead of Frank.

Before he could reach them, he was overtaken by an unmarked police car. In it were Chief Collig and Mr. Hardy, with Officer Riley at the wheel. Frank quickly jumped in.

Knowing the neighborhood well, Collig surmised that Chipman was on his way to a rooming house near the corner of the block. It was the only one on the street.

"Fenton," he said, "I think it's best to grab him

before he gets there. Once he's inside with that .45, it'll be difficult to capture him and somebody might get hurt.

"We'll go around the block quickly and cut through the back yard, then hide behind the house next to the rooming house. I'll radio Johnston and Carroll who are riding ahead of us and tell them to creep up on Chipman. When they get near, they're to jump out of the car and cover him from behind while I take him from the front. Riley, you cover for me."

"Right," said Riley, and drove the car to the designated spot.

"Watch yourself," Mr. Hardy said to the chief. "The force needs you."

"Don't worry," Collig replied grimly. "I have a score to settle with that scoundrel!"

He radioed Johnston and Carroll and outlined his plan of action. Then he and Riley got out and flattened themselves against the building, with revolvers in hand.

Mr. Hardy and Frank also left the car and watched the scene from a distance. Chipman came into view, carrying his groceries in his left arm. A long cigar hung jauntily from his mouth.

Collig and Riley walked up to him. "Raise your hands!" the chief commanded.

Chipman dropped the bag and drew a pistol from his hip pocket. But he never had a chance to use it because the chief's gun spoke first. Chipman spun around with a bullet in his shoulder and fell to the sidewalk. The .45 caliber automatic clattered beside

The chief's gun spoke first

him. In an instant he was grabbed by Johnston and Carroll, who kicked away the pistol and handcuffed the prisoner.

The hardened criminal began to whine, "Don't shoot any more, I'm dying!"

The chief answered grimly, "No, you're not. And you got a better break than you gave my nephew!"

The killer's wound proved to be superficial. While he was given first aid by the police, Chief Collig advised him of his constitutional right to consult a lawyer before making any statement. Chipman, however, volunteered the information that his two buddies were living in the rooming house. He also told the officers that the men were unarmed and that the bank loot was in a paper bag in the bureau.

The chief and his men, nevertheless, took proper precautions upon entering the house, their revolvers ready in case they had to use them. They arrested the other two robbers without any trouble. The bank's money was recovered, except for a small amount that the men had spent.

In a written confession obtained later, Chipman admitted shooting Officer Tom Collig. The bank robbers were on the way to their rooming house when Collig saw the speeding car approaching. He let it pass, then turned around to give chase. That was when Chipman whizzed around a curve and sideswiped the pole. Collig caught up to the sedan and Chipman stopped.

He said that at first the officer was only going to give him a summons. But when he found that Chipman had no owner's registration, Tom Collig ordered him to follow his motorcycle to headquarters. Chipman offered the policeman a bribe, which Collig had indignantly spurned. When the officer turned to mount his cycle, Chipman had shot him in the back.

That evening, after the criminals had been locked up, Frank, Joe, and Chet gathered in Mr. Hardy's study to discuss the highlights of the case. "What I don't understand," said Chet, "is why Chipman wore the adhesive tape when he held up the bank."

"That's easy," Joe answered. "He has a large mole over his right eye, remember? Realizing that this would identify him, he covered it with the piece of adhesive tape. Right, Dad?"

"Exactly. That kind of thing has been done many times. There are also some cases on record where a criminal had no facial scar or mark, but added adhesive tape to some part of his face to confuse an observer."

"You and the boys," said Chet, "have taught me a lot about observation. Now I know it's the keystone to the success of any criminal investigation."

"True," Mr. Hardy replied. "And you've caught on fast. If you hadn't spotted Chipman on the street, we would still be looking for him."

"Yes, Dad," Frank said with a grin. "But that's the first time I've ever heard of anyone solving a case while sitting on a curb!"

CHAPTER VI

THE CLUE OF THE BROKEN PENCIL

Search of Crime Scene and Suspect

"AFTER a crime has been committed, the investigator must go to the scene as quickly as possible to make a search of the location."

The pleasant voice was that of Fenton Hardy. He was seated in his study with Frank and Joe, and instructing their pal Chet on the subject of crime scene searches.

The detective continued, "The collection and preservation of physical evidence and clues to be used by investigators in solving a crime are of greatest importance. The evidence must be properly collected and preserved to meet the legal requirements allowing its use in court when the case is tried.

"Now, Frank," Mr. Hardy said, "tell Chet what has to be done at a crime scene."

"The basic rule," replied the dark-haired boy, "is to protect the scene. This means that no one is allowed to enter the area, except the officers who will process it for evidence. Entry of the crime scene by other persons may result in destroying, altering, moving important evidence, or in leaving new items or marks which could mislead the investigators.

"Next, the crime scene is recorded. The best way to start is by photographing the scene. Then sketches of it are made, and finally casts of shoe and tire prints after they have been properly photographed. Also, fingerprints have to be photographed and lifted."

Frank paused, then continued, "Probably the most important duty of the investigator is to make notes of all observations, evidence located, photographed and collected. It's good practice to have one officer in charge of the crime scene search who will take notes and direct the search in a systematic manner. He will witness the location of each piece of evidence and will initial it together with the officer who discovered and preserved it. Both should also initial the notes. This way either of them can later testify in court."

"It sounds complicated," Chet remarked. "And a lot of equipment is needed."

"Not really," answered Joe. "Look at this."

He leaned over and picked up an attache case. In it were an ordinary camera with a flash-bulb attachment, extra bulbs and film, a clipboard with a pad of graph paper, note paper, and an engineer's scale. Also included were assorted pencils, a steel tape measure, rubber gloves, assorted empty pillboxes, plain envelopes, cellophane envelopes of various sizes, Scotch tape, evidence stickers, and a compass.

"We call this the Hardy Crime Scene Kit," Joe told Chet.

Frank spoke up. "One reason we photograph a scene is for the presentation of the pictures to a judge or jury so they can easily visualize what happened, and to settle any questions they may have in their minds concerning the crime scene."

"In other words," Chet said, "you make photos from different angles."

"Right. We use a wide-angle lens first, then make close-ups of all important pieces of evidence."

"Very good," said Mr. Hardy. "Joe, suppose you tell Chet now about sketching the crime scene."

"Sure," Joe replied. "Chet, first we have to decide what type of sketch would be most useful. It's also important to obtain an overall impression. For example, if the crime scene is outdoors, we must figure out how much ground to cover. There's no sense in bringing in the entire countryside if it's not important."

Chet chuckled. But he became serious again as Joe continued.

"To record the location of evidence believed to be important, we have to decide what base line to use and if necessary what fixed points. Then we measure the exact distance from these fixed points. The evidence will be charted on the graph paper."

Joe stressed that all measurements must be accurate. Where the distance is great, the investigator may use pacing or an automobile speedometer. To make sure that measurements are exact, more than one officer should check the tape measure.

"In almost every sketch," Joe said, "you have to use a scale. And—"

"Wait a minute. What do you mean by a scale?"

"Well, it's usually not possible to get a sheet of paper big enough to show the true measurements. So we scale it down. For instance, we'll make one-half inch equal to a foot. Or we use whatever scale we think is necessary in order to incorporate the measurements needed. This goes for both indoor and outdoor locations."

"I see. Go on," Chet said.

Frank took up the explanation. "On the sketch we show the exact location, according to scale, of all important evidence—the approaches and entrances to the room or the area, the size of the area, and the position of windows or doors.

"Other things to be recorded," Frank said, "are the title, which is a brief descriptive heading, for example 'Homicide of John Doe,' the address or location, an arrow pointing north, the date the sketch was made and who made it."

"In order not to clutter the sketch with writing," Mr. Hardy pointed out, "symbols and numbers are used in the legend. The general rule is to use letters for furniture and fixed articles, and numbers for items of evidence."

Joe, who was watching Chet nod his head, said mischievously, "How about rectangular coordinates and triangulations?"

Chet grinned. "I'll take a dozen."

"We use those two methods," Frank said, "to pin-point evidence on a sketch. We usually take the rectangular coordinates where we have rectangular lines. For instance, the walls of a room. In order to locate the evidence, we draw a dotted line from it to any side; then at right angles to this line and from the evidence we draw another line to an adjoining side. The—"

"Wait a minute," interjected Mr. Hardy. "This whole thing must sound like Greek to Chet. Suppose you take this piece of paper and illustrate it by drawing as you talk."

"Okay, Dad," Frank said and drew a sketch.

"See?" he said to Chet. "We identify the violation, the residence, the room, show the date, our initials, and the compass reading of north. Then we indicate the corners of the room with capital letters, and the location of the evidence as *1*. Next we draw perpendicular lines to the west and south walls which intersect at *1*. This graphically locates *1* in the room and

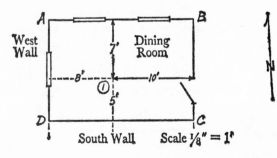

SKETCH 1

permits us to relocate *1* at any time in the future by making the same two simple measurements."

"I get it," said Chet. "Actually, the dotted lines you drew are coordinates, each parallel with walls that meet so if you measured north on the west wall from corner *D* five feet, and east from *D* on the south wall eight feet, the lines or coordinates drawn perpendicular to these points would intersect at *1* or where the evidence was located."

"That's right, Chet," said Mr. Hardy.

"I learned it in math class," Chet remarked.

"Now I'll tell you about triangulation," continued Frank. "It is probably the most useful method of locating a specific point. It can be applied indoors, but is usually applied in outdoor crime scenes. It is based on locating two permanent fixed points from which the location of a third temporary point is determined.

"For example, in this sketch, we know that the corners, the doorway, the heating vents or radiators are fixed points. Therefore, if we measured corners *D* and *C* to point *1*, that point can always be relocated with respect to *D* and *C*.

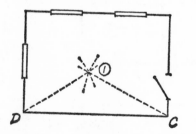

SKETCH **2**

"Let me illustrate this further." Frank made another sketch.

"You see," he went on, "point *1* is the only place at which lines *C* and *D* will intersect within the room using the original measured length for each line.

"Now let's consider the application of triangulation outdoors. We must always select two permanent points of reference, similar to the corners *D* and *C* in the sketch that I just made. Some of the better outdoor reference points are survey marks, fire hydrants, and drain sewers, because records of their location are maintained by local and county agencies. Utility poles are excellent, too. And, of course, there are other points. It's up to the investigator to pick the best ones."

Frank quickly drew a third sketch.

"You see," he went on, "to locate the evidence on this drawing, we simply measure south from utility

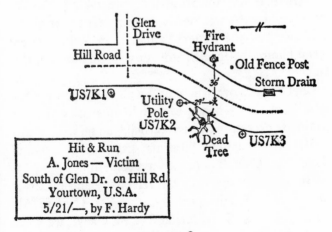

SKETCH 3

pole number US7K2 to X and westward from the fire hydrant to X. An experienced investigator would never select either the old fence post or the dead tree as a reference point, because they may soon rot away or be removed.

"In this case it would be hard to draw to scale. However, the sketch can be reproduced on a scale map of the area prepared by the municipality or county."

Mr. Hardy had been looking over Frank's shoulder.

"Very good, son," he commented. To Chet he said, "Remember, every investigator must carry a notebook and pencil. He must never rely on memory. From the minute he arrives at the scene he should be busy writing, recording the time of day, date, location, weather and details of the area, people present, and anything else that he believes pertinent to the investigation.

"There is no substitute for note taking. For instance, when the weather is an important part of the evidence and the camera cannot show it in a crime scene photo, the investigator must make notes on this fact."

Chet sighed, overwhelmed by all the new information. "I wish we had a case right now in which we could use everything I just learned," he said.

Mr. Hardy smiled. "You may get your wish one of these days, Chet. There's always something—"

He was interrupted by the telephone and picked it up. "Fenton Hardy speaking. . . . Yes, Captain Abbott. . . . Yes, I understand. . . . Okay, we'll be right there." He hung up and turned to the boys.

"A big burglary at the Rex Manufacturing Company on the edge of town. Make sure all the equipment is in the car. Chet, you're getting your wish already!"

On the way to the Rex company, the detective told the boys that Chief Collig was on vacation and Captain Abbott was acting in his place.

"Seven thousand five hundred dollars in cash and about as much in gold and silver have been stolen from Rex," Mr. Hardy added, "by a person or persons who had gained entry through a window which had been broken."

The Hardys and their friend were met outside the building by Captain Abbott and the president of the firm, Charles Willets, who was pale and shaken.

Mr. Willets said to Mr. Hardy, "Please help me. This will ruin our business. Our insurance is not sufficient to cover this loss."

"We'll do everything in our power to find the burglars," Mr. Hardy assured the man. "Tell us what happened."

"Last night," Mr. Willets began, "I left the office later than usual after everyone was gone. I was checking on some shipments. Business had been slow but was just beginning to improve. I hurried home because I expected guests for dinner. They stayed late, but after they left my mind went back to business. Suddenly I was not sure whether I had closed the safe. I often forgot before, but never worried because there was little cash on hand. Yesterday, however, I did business with a new firm for the first time. When I checked their credit rating, I insisted upon payment in cash. That's the reason I had so much here."

He continued, "About two o'clock this morning I drove to the factory. I thought I saw a light flash in the office as I approached, but then dismissed the idea, thinking my imagination was playing tricks."

Mr. Willets stopped to mop his forehead, then went on:

"I unlocked the door and reached for the light switch. Two men suddenly jumped on me. They bound me with rope hand and foot and gagged me. Then they threw me in that old closet at the end of the hall. I didn't see their faces, because my eyes had not grown accustomed to the dark. I know that one of them was huge and strong. I could tell by the way he handled me.

"It's a big closet with a strong lock. We used to keep gold and silver in it before we built a bigger storeroom."

"Why do you keep precious metals here?" inquired Captain Abbott.

"We make gold and silver eyeglass frames."

"Of course," Mr. Hardy said. "Please tell us more."

"Well," Mr. Willets continued, "I lay there for hours. Finally my secretary arrived for work and opened the door. She called one of the workers and he untied me. I checked the safe. It was open and the money was gone. None of the desks had been ransacked and everything else seemed to be in order.

"Then I suddenly remembered the gold and silver. I went to the security room. It had been broken open.

One look inside and I could see that the metal had been stolen."

"What has been done so far?" Mr. Hardy asked Captain Abbott.

"The crime scene has been protected. Higgins is taking photographs right now."

"Good. Let's go inside." Fenton Hardy beckoned the three boys to follow him. Then he paused in the doorway and seemed to be taking a mental picture of the room. He whipped out his notebook and jotted something down.

"Chet," he said, "there's no better time to learn than right now. Joe, bring the crime scene kit in, will you? Give Chet a clipboard, some paper, a notebook, and pencil and go to work. On second thought, you and Chet go outside and make a sketch of the window which was smashed by the burglars and whatever else seems relevant."

Mr. Hardy also took a clipboard and placed graph paper on it. Then he helped Captain Abbott and Frank to measure the location of essential evidence in the room. When they were finished, the captain asked Officer Rinshaw to dust for prints.

Fenton Hardy now went to the storeroom from which the gold and silver had been stolen. He looked about, but found no clue.

As he left the room, he asked Mr. Willets, "Are there any containers missing in which the metal might have been carried out?"

"Oh," Mr. Willets replied, "they took it in the chest it was stored in."

"Hm!" Mr. Hardy said thoughtfully. "Please give me a description of it."

He made notes as Mr. Willets replied that the box was made of steel, about two feet deep, four feet long, and one foot wide. It had handles on each end and was locked with a key.

"How about the color?" the detective asked.

"Steel gray."

Just then Chet rushed up. "Mr. Hardy, we found the tool which was used to smash the window! Come with me!" Chet led the way to the street and pointed to the gutter. In it lay a pick handle.

"Nice going, Chet. Photograph it and sketch it on your graph paper. Then it will be dusted for prints by Rinshaw and secured for evidence."

Mr. Hardy turned to the captain and said, "We'll be glad to help you make a crime scene search outdoors."

"Fine," the captain said, and ordered his men to line up across the street from the factory and spread out about an arm's length apart.

"We'll walk up to the building," he said, "go around it, and then line up the same way on the other side."

"Chet," said Mr. Hardy, "let me give you a few basic rules that must be obeyed. The most important thing is search discipline. Everyone must observe everything around him on the ground or in trees very carefully. The men will walk abreast of each other, in a straight line. Only in this way can a proper systematic search be conducted. Any questions?"

"What are they going to look for?" Chet asked.

"Just about anything, including shoe prints."

Captain Abbott was instructing his men as the Hardys and Chet joined them. "If you locate something," he said, "hold up your hand to attract attention. Don't touch it."

"The reason for this," Mr. Hardy told Chet, "is that its location must be charted on a sketch, and if it's an article that the thieves might have dropped, it has to be dusted for fingerprints."

Now the line of policemen went about the search. The turning point would be just beyond a small ridge about two hundred feet in the woods, which stretched behind the Rex Manufacturing Company.

As they neared the edge of the woods, Chet Morton held up his hand and yelled excitedly, "Here! Here!"

"What is it?" Captain Abbott asked.

"A broken pencil. Maybe it doesn't mean anything—"

"Even a seemingly insignificant article may turn out to be a vital clue," Captain Abbott told him. "Good work, Chet!"

Mr. Hardy made a note, marked the location of the yellow pencil in his sketch, then picked it up.

The search party went on. They had almost reached the turning point when Joe suddenly shouted from a patch of woods, "Here it is!"

Mr. Hardy and Captain Abbott quickly walked to the location. On the ground lay the stolen metal chest. Joe removed the broken branches which partly concealed it and found it still intact.

Mr. Hardy and Captain Abbott decided that all the officers would be instructed to maintain silence concerning the discovery of the chest. Most of them were sent to their routine duties.

Officer Rinshaw carefully dusted the chest for latent fingerprints. Many were found, and after they had been photographed and lifted, the chest was removed to police headquarters.

An identical chest was obtained from the local hardware store, filled with rocks, and placed where the stolen chest had been discovered. Chet was full of curiosity. "What's going on, fellows?" he asked.

"Dad and Captain Abbott are going to set up what is termed *a plant*," Joe replied. "Police will be detailed to watch and see if an attempt is made to pick up the phony chest."

"That's right, Chet," joined in Mr. Hardy. "Two officers will be hidden in the shrubbery at all times, and if someone comes for the chest, he'll be apprehended. Now, I think we'd better go to the Police Identification Division to see if Rinshaw has come up with anything."

Upon their arrival at headquarters, Rinshaw informed Mr. Hardy and Captain Abbott that there were several sets of prints on the chest. He had found upon comparison that some were Mr. Willets'. However, he was unable to make any other identification. He also told them there were some latent prints on the pick handle that matched the unidentifiable ones on the chest.

Mr. Hardy nodded, then read over his notes. Chet

approached him. "Would you look at my sketch, Mr. Hardy?"

"Sure." The detective took the boy's chart and examined it. Suddenly he exclaimed, "Chet, do you mean to tell me there's a lot of broken glass on the outside of this window?"

"That's right. A lot of it. Why?"

Mr. Hardy did not answer but looked at his own sketch carefully. Then he said in a surprised voice, "That's odd. It looks as if the window was smashed from the inside. I wonder—" His voice trailed off in silence. Then he studied his sons' sketches.

"Frank," he asked, "how about this car near the curb down the street?"

"I saw it parked there," Frank replied. "So I placed it on the chart."

"Too bad we didn't pay attention to it sooner," Mr. Hardy remarked. "Do you have any notes on it?"

Frank took out his pad, and after scanning it he said, "The hood was up. I wrote down the license number."

Mr. Hardy turned to the captain. "It's just a hunch, but we'd better check with the Motor Vehicle Bureau and find out who owns the car."

Abbott nodded and had one of his officers send out a teletype.

Frank, meanwhile, continued to scan his notes. Then he said, "During our search, a wrecker from the Triangle Towing Service hoisted the front end of the car. I saw a man talking with the mechanic."

"I think we ought to follow this up," Mr. Hardy

said. "Captain, let s take a ride to the towing service. Come on, boys."

At the Triangle Garage Captain Abbott did most of the talking. From the mechanic they learned that he had received a call requesting that he tow a car from the vicinity of the Rex company. When he arrived there, he recognized the automobile as belonging to William Tiller, the firm's bookkeeper. Tiller asked him to find the cause of the trouble. After a brief examination, the mechanic told him that the coil was not functioning. He offered to pick up a new one and replace it. But the bookkeeper insisted that he tow the car to the garage at once, even though he would have to pay a towing fee.

Tiller waited for his car to be repaired. He was obviously in a hurry and explained that Mr. Willets wanted him to make an important trip. He had the tank filled and the oil checked. After paying the bill, he departed quickly.

When the mechanic had finished, Fenton Hardy walked over to the telephone booth. He dialed a number and spoke rapidly to someone. Then he told the others, "I talked to Mr. Willets. He said Tiller disappeared from the office just before we started the search. Willets did not pay much attention to the fact and emphasized that Tiller is a trusted employee. He had a key to the office door and obviously often worked on the books at night. Mr. Willets denied, however, that he had sent the man on a trip. Tiller lives in a furnished room at 12 West Street. Let's go over and talk to him right away."

They were proceeding toward West Street when Frank said, "Look! There's the car that was parked down the street from the Rex company. It's coming toward us!"

"Let it pass then turn around quick!" Captain Abbott ordered his driver.

"The man who's driving is the one I saw talking to the mechanic!" Frank cried out.

"No doubt it's Tiller," muttered Captain Abbott. "He sure is in a hurry."

Tiller poured on the gas.

"Captain," said Mr. Hardy, "let's give him the siren so he'll stop!"

The shrieking sound had the opposite effect on Tiller. He increased his speed. But the squad car gained. Finally the skillful driving of the police chauffeur convinced Tiller that escape was impossible and he came to a stop on the shoulder of the road. As the police car halted slightly to the rear, the officer driving opened his door and covered Tiller from behind it with his service revolver. Captain Abbott, with gun drawn, cautiously approached the suspect's car from the right rear.

He ordered in a loud, clear voice, "Put your hands over your head!"

Tiller obeyed. The police chauffeur walked toward the suspect's car and swung open the driver's door. "Keep your hands on your head and step out," he said. Then he told Tiller to face his car and side-step to the right until he stood next to the police sedan.

"Keep your hands on your head!" Captain Abbott
ordered

Tiller, a slight man, reluctantly complied, his shrewd eyes dartingly examining the situation. He was obviously seeking some avenue of escape.

Captain Abbott holstered his weapon and said, "Tiller, make no move unless I tell you to. Now slowly place your hands on the edge of the car roof and spread them as far apart as possible. All right. Now shuffle your feet back as far as you can, and spread them apart."

After the suspect had complied, Captain Abbott hooked his left foot in front of Tiller's left foot and forced his legs even farther apart. This placed Tiller off balance and gave him a minimum chance to turn and assault the police officer.

The chauffeur moved slightly behind Tiller, gun in hand. He stationed himself in a way so that Captain Abbott would not be in the line of fire if the suspect made an attempt to get away.

Frank, Joe, and Chet were watching from inside the police car as Captain Abbott began to search the suspect.

"Chet," Frank said, "this is called the wall search. It is a preliminary search and the officer looks for drugs or weapons the suspect might use to injure himself or the officer. Once the suspect is in this position, with his hands on a car or against a wall, the officer begins either on the right or the left side. Captain Abbott is starting on the left. When he goes to the right, you will note that he'll walk behind the chauffeur so as not to pass between the suspect and the gun."

Chet nodded and Frank went on, "Here's what you do step by step:

1. Slide your left foot in front of the suspect's left leg and inside his left foot. Exert a slight knee pressure against the front of his leg. When you search the right side, you use your right foot. This position will enable you to sense and counteract a movement by the suspect.

2. Search the suspect's headgear.

3. Examine mouth, nose, ear, hair, and palm of left hand.

4. Start at left wrist and with both hands feel for any foreign object which might be in the suspect's clothing or strapped to his skin. Probe to the shoulder.

5. Search around his shoulder, around his neck, the front portion of his body, the side of his body, and his back. Pay special attention to the area between his shoulder blades and the small of his back. Often knives are strapped in the hollow areas.

6. Search his waistline by removing his belt and examining the inside of his trouser waistband.

7. Search in the groin area and down the suspect's left leg, pull his sock down and feel inside his shoe top.

8. Repeat the same procedure on the suspect's other side. Some areas will overlap.

9. Empty all pockets.

"One more thing," Frank added. "Don't pat, but

feel your way over the suspect's body. This way thin, flat objects won't be missed."

"What do you do with the stuff you find?" Chet asked.

"Whatever is convenient," Frank said. "Weapons you retain on your person, other items you put on the roof of the car or on the ground. Later they are placed in an envelope or bag.

"After the search, you handcuff your man and take him to headquarters. There he will be subjected to a very thorough strip search and his clothing will be examined carefully."

"Suppose you don't have a second officer available to cover the suspect with his gun while you search?" Chet asked.

"Then you hold your gun in one hand while searching with the other," Frank said.

"What if you have two prisoners?"

"In that case one must be flat on his stomach with his arms extended forward, palms flat on the ground. Then you conduct your search in the method I just described. When you're finished with the first suspect, you handcuff him, force him to lie down, and search the other man."

While Frank had been talking, Captain Abbott had removed a fully loaded automatic from Tiller's belt and handed it to his colleague. When the prisoner was handcuffed, a careful search was made of the car.

"You've got nothing on me, copper," Tiller snarled, "except carrying that gun and I can explain that."

No one made any comment. The car yielded no clues, and the captain appeared puzzled.

"Did you find anything important beside the gun?" Mr. Hardy asked.

"No. All he has on him is a wallet with personal credit cards, some bills, change, a comb, a ballpoint pen, and a broken pencil."

"A broken pencil?" Chet shouted excitedly.

All looked up in surprise. Captain Abbott caught on and said, "Of course. I forgot all about that. This broken pencil is yellow just like the other one, and I'll bet all the tea in China that it will match that piece we found."

Mr. Hardy opened the trunk of the car again. After looking around carefully, he leaned on the spare tire and found that it was not inflated. He took it out and forced it away from the rim. Everyone gasped! A mass of bills and checks spilled out!

"Wow!" Chet's eyes bulged in amazement. "Who would have thought of that!"

Tiller was advised of his constitutional rights as an arrested person, and then taken to police headquarters. The others followed. Here they learned that the policemen hidden in the woods had apprehended a man named Ford Williams when he attempted to pick up the steel chest.

Williams had already confessed his part in the crime. He had known Tiller in New York City. Both had criminal records and had been in jail together. About five years ago the two men had committed a burglary. Williams was apprehended, but Tiller escaped. The bookkeeper, whose real name was Hans Shinner, had used the alias of William Tiller and had come to Bayport. Shortly after his arrival he was employed by Mr. Willets.

Williams had served almost five years for his crime. Upon being released, he had been contacted by Tiller, who told him that Willets was an easy target and that the town's police were "hicks."

The previous night he had received a telephone call from Tiller to come to Bayport immediately. He told Williams that he had staked out the factory, waited till Mr. Willets left, and made sure that the safe had been left open.

The two burglars had entered the building with Tiller's key and rifled the unlocked safe. They had just broken the lock on the storeroom door when they noticed the glare of oncoming headlights. Then Mr. Willets opened the door and reached for the light switch.

The powerful Williams seized him. He was bound and thrown into the closet. In order to give the impression of a forced entry, Tiller smashed the window from inside the building with a pick handle. When they left, after locking the door again, Tiller threw the pick handle in the gutter.

The thieves had loaded the chest into Tiller's car. It had refused to start. Tiller became panic-stricken at the thought of leaving the chest containing the gold and silver in the car at the scene. So he and Williams carried the chest to the woods. Then they deflated Tiller's spare tire and stuffed the currency and checks inside.

Williams had gone to a hotel for the rest of the

night and the following day. It was planned that the car would be repaired and the chest picked up that evening after working hours. Then the two men would leave Bayport.

Tiller, however, changed his mind when he realized that the employees would obviously be questioned by the police. He had tried to have his car picked up before daybreak, but had no luck. The Triangle Garage had promised to send a man early in the morning. Tiller waited, but the man did not show up before the company opened. He went to work, keeping an eye on the car. When the tow truck arrived, he slipped out, had the car removed, and was planning to leave town without Williams as soon as the repairs were finished.

Williams, in turn, was unable to reach Tiller by telephone and had become suspicious. He had returned alone to the spot where they had left the chest, and walked right into the arms of the police.

Captain Abbott commented, "This illustrates the old saying, 'There's no honor among thieves!' "

The next morning the three Hardys and Chet Morton were again seated in Mr. Hardy's study. All were in good humor, chatting about their exploits of the previous day.

"I think Chet has graduated from the recruit class," Mr. Hardy said with a twinkle. Then he added, "Chet, I'm proud of you. Be ready to help us solve the next mystery!"

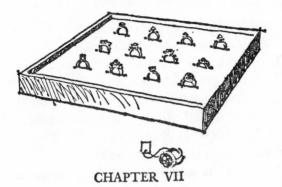

CHAPTER VII

THE TRAIL BEYOND THE SMOKE SCREEN

Surveillance

FENTON HARDY was pacing his room in a large hotel in Newark, New Jersey, when a knock sounded on the door. He opened it. Outside stood Frank and Joe and their chum Chet Morton.

"Hi, Dad!" Joe said, grinning. "Surprised to see us?"

"Sure am," Mr. Hardy replied.

"Mother told us you were here," Frank said, "and we drove down. You've been on this assignment for nine days, and we thought there might be something we could do."

"Thanks." The detective smiled. But then a frown clouded his face. "This is really a tough case. I'm up against the wall!"

"Can we help you?" Chet asked.

"I'm afraid not," Mr. Hardy replied.

"Can you tell us about it?" Frank inquired.

Mr. Hardy nodded. "I've been engaged by a famous national jewelry corporation to investigate the theft of thousands of dollars' worth of merchandise from their showroom in New York City. The trail led to Newark. The police here are cooperating as much as they can, even though the actual crime took place in another state.

"So far, the police have located seven pieces of the stolen jewelry in Newark pawnshops. The pawnbrokers recorded the name, address, and physical description of the person who pawned them. The names and addresses in all cases were the same and proved to be fictitious. But a comparison of descriptions confirms my—and the police's—suspicion about the thief's identity."

"Who is he?" Frank wanted to know.

"A junior officer of the jewelry company."

"Then why hasn't he been arrested?" Joe asked.

"We decided to hold off and try to recover the jewelry. The police go along with me in my plans. I must find out where it is and also make sure that the suspect is the actual thief."

"Why don't you tail him, Mr. Hardy?" Chet asked.

"He knows me by sight. I've tried using other detectives, but no luck. This guy's clever and suspicious."

There was a moment of gloomy silence. Then Joe said, "Why don't you give us a chance at it, Dad? He'd never suspect that we boys were tailing him."

"That's right," Frank broke in enthusiastically. "You know, we've done surveillance in almost every case we worked on."

Mr. Hardy thought for a moment, then said, "You know, this might not be a bad idea!"

"Great!" Frank said. "Let's get started."

"Wait a minute. The first thing you'll have to do is call Mother. Tell her you're spending a couple of days with me. Chet also had better call home."

The boys grinned. "We've told her already. Mrs. Morton too." Frank explained.

"Oh?" Mr. Hardy kept a straight face. Then he phoned the desk clerk and obtained an adjoining room for the boys.

After a quick lunch in the hotel's restaurant, they all went to Mr. Hardy's room to plan their strategy.

"I'll tell you all the important aspects of the case," Mr. Hardy said. "Ask questions any time."

He settled in a lounge chair and began. "Ten days ago there was a fire in the company's store in New York City. It flared up suddenly in a bundle of cleaning rags stored in a large closet under a stairway. It was a heavy, smoke-laden fire which spread rapidly. Customers and employees fled to the street. Someone tried the fire extinguisher near the closet, but it didn't work and he called the fire department. It was a stubborn blaze, but they confined it to the stairway area and finally put it out."

Mr. Hardy glanced from one boy to another and went on, "All the personnel returned to the store afterward. At first it was believed that the fire had been caused by paints and chemicals stored in the closet. But the fire chief was suspicious. He called the Arson Squad to make an investigation."

The trio listened intently as Mr. Hardy continued.

"That evening, when the employees began to lock up the jewelry, one of the most trusted salesmen reported the disappearance of an entire tray of diamond jewelry. It was valued at more than $100,000. The police, the FBI, and the insurance company were immediately notified, and liaison will be maintained.

"The search of the premises by the Arson Squad and detectives turned up the missing tray, which was partially consumed, inside the burned closet. But none of the jewelry was found. Samples of ashes, remnants of rags, and other burned material were taken to the laboratory for examination, as well as a glassine envelope which contained traces of a white powder. The envelope was found in a wastepaper basket in the men's room.

"The next day another minute search of the store for the jewelry was made and proved unsuccessful. It was at that time that the Arson Squad notified Kenneth Craig, the president of the concern, that the fire had been deliberately set. The lab examination determined that the rags had been impregnated with paints and gasoline before the fire was started.

"Also, it was found that the substance in the glassine envelope was heroin. As a result, the New York City Police Department Narcotics Bureau entered the case. It was at that point that I was called into the case by Mr. Craig."

"What did you do first?" Frank asked.

"I interviewed every employee and officer of the company as well as every customer present when the fire started, and all the firemen who fought the blaze."

"The firemen too!" Chet exclaimed in surprise. "I would have never thought of that."

"We ruled out the firemen as possible suspects," Mr. Hardy continued, "because none of them had been near the section from which the jewels were missing."

"But, Dad," interrupted Frank, "how about the clerk in charge of the section where the jewelry was stolen? Didn't he notice anything unusual?"

"I'm coming to that. His name is Jerome Dempster. He told us that he had just put that particular tray back into the showcase when the fire was discovered. He hurried to the closet in an effort to put out the blaze with the fire extinguisher, but it did not work. He subsequently called the fire department. Then he tried to go back to the closet, but was blinded by the smoke and forced to move to the street door.

"He remembered seeing Ronald Lackey, a junior vice-president in the company, near his section when the fire started. Later, when he looked back from the exit, he thought he noticed Lackey near the closet, but was not sure because of the smoke."

"Excuse me, Dad," cut in Joe, "but have you made a background investigation of the staff?"

"Yes. I've checked to see if there was anyone with a police record, but the results were negative. I also checked credit companies and neighbors and found

Dempster was blinded by the smoke

out that all the personnel live conventional lives with the possible exception of Ronald Lackey, who owes large sums of money."

"But, Mr. Hardy," burst out Chet, "you said that he's an officer of the company. How could he be the thief?"

"Well, my boy," the detective said, "just because Lackey's a vice-president doesn't necessarily mean he's honest. All I know is what the evidence indicates. I haven't said that he stole the jewels, but I'm sure he pawned some of them."

"You mean the pawnbrokers' description of their customer fits him?"

"Right. I showed them his photograph and three of the shopkeepers were pretty sure that Lackey was the man who pawned the jewels."

"Dad, you're great," Frank said admiringly. "But why did you suspect him in the first place?"

"Well, he had some rather large debts. Then I found out that he was dismissed from college for stealing money from the room of a fellow student. The student didn't press charges, so Lackey has no police record.

"I also found out by a search of court records that his wife was recently granted a divorce on a charge of desertion. At the present time he is living alone in a studio apartment in the suburbs of Newark. He doesn't have to pay alimony and has only himself to support. His salary is considerable and I wondered why all these debts."

Frank nodded. "It certainly seems odd."

"How long has he been an officer of Towers?" Joe asked.

"About two years. You see, it's this way. Ronald Lackey's father married Mr. Craig's sister. They started a jewelry company, worked hard, and prospered. About three years ago Lackey's father got him the job with the firm, even though Mr. Craig, his uncle, was not too happy about it. For about a year Lackey was the public-relations manager for the company and did very well. He was married that year.

"Because of his good record and, I suppose, some influence of his father, he was made a junior vice-president. Soon after that his troubles began. He had difficulties with his marriage, began to drink, gambled, and kept questionable company.

"His father was forced to pay his debts to avoid a scandal. About eight months ago his father died. There was hardly any estate left because of his son's demands. Mr. Craig is disgusted with his nephew, but keeps him in the firm to avoid hurting his sister, who has been ill for a long time."

"He sure sounds like an unstable character," Joe said. "Let's go to work on him right away. How about searching his apartment?"

"Yes, Dad," Frank put in. "Certainly the information from the pawnbrokers would be sufficient to obtain a warrant?"

"None of them made a positive identification."

Mr. Hardy got up, paced around the room, and continued. "I interviewed Lackey's former wife. She told me that her husband had started to use marijuana shortly after their marriage. She believes that he's using stronger drugs and thinks he buys them from a young man named Dale Britt who came to their apartment for short visits prior to their separation. Mrs. Lackey identified a Newark police mug shot of Dale Britt as the man. Also, the doorman at Lackey's apartment house identified Dale Britt's photograph as that of a frequent caller, who had stopped his visits only recently."

"Boy," Frank said, "this will be a dangerous assignment if it involves narcotic addicts."

"Right," Mr. Hardy agreed. "For this reason I want

you to be very careful. I'm not sure that Lackey is an addict, but I strongly suspect it. He seems the type who could easily become a victim of this terrible kind of slavery. I can't think of a worse fate to befall any human being! An addict will steal or commit other crimes, even murder, to get the stuff!"

The three boys sat in silence on the edges of their chairs, staring at the detective. They had never seen him so aroused about any subject.

Finally Mr. Hardy pulled an envelope from his coat pocket and took out two photographs. "This is Lackey, and that's Britt. Study the pictures well so you will recognize these men immediately."

Frank, Joe, and Chet followed his advice and passed the photographs around. Ronald Lackey was a homely man of twenty-nine, slight of build, with an obstinate expression. He had thinning light hair, large protruding ears, a hawk nose, beady eyes, thin lips, a receding chin, and a prominent Adam's apple.

The other photo showed a young man about twenty-three years old, slender, with long wavy hair and prominent sideburns. He had a low brow, deep-set eyes, a long, thin nose, large mouth, and a sharp chin.

"Dale Britt is a convicted heroin addict," Mr. Hardy explained. "He also has a criminal record dating back to his teens for purse snatching, burglary, and auto theft. He is wanted right now by the police as a parole violator."

"Quite a record," Joe muttered.

"Hm!" Mr. Hardy said. "Now here's where you come in. I've learned that Lackey leaves his office in

New York about five P.M. He generally eats a very light dinner in a small restaurant near the store. Sometimes he doesn't eat at all.

"Then he takes a train which leaves him off about a half mile from his apartment. He sold his car recently and walks home."

"And what does he do at night?" Frank asked.

"I'm coming to that. Lately he never has any company. He goes out every night, but at no specific time. Some evenings he departs a few minutes after he gets home, while other times he leaves late."

"Do you know where he goes?" Frank asked.

"He takes a bus to Newark and always gets off at the same intersection. This is where my operatives have failed in their surveillance. They have never been able to follow him to his destination. He has used every trick to lose them—he has stopped at a store and doubled back, pretended to wait for a bus, and has used other similar tactics. He seems to sense that he's being tailed. When he becomes suspicious he'll jump onto a bus or hail a taxi. Anyway, he disappears, and then returns to his apartment very late."

"But, Mr. Hardy," Chet said with a frown, "do you have any idea whom he goes to see?"

"I suspect that he's visiting Dale Britt. But I have no facts to substantiate this."

"How about staking out Dale's house?" Joe suggested.

"The police do not know where Britt lives."

"Where do we go from here, then?" Frank asked.

Joe spoke up. "In tailing Lackey, I think the three-man surveillance would be the best."

"Right, Joe," chimed in Frank. "Don't you agree, Dad?"

"Sure do. You'll start tonight."

"Wait a minute," said Chet. "I don't know how three-man surveillance works."

"I'll explain it to you," Frank said. "It's easy. The procedure in this type of shadowing is for three detectives to be scattered near the place where they expect to see the suspect. The first sleuth walks a reasonable distance behind him. The second follows the first and, in turn, the third follows the second.

"Any time the first detective feels that he is suspected, he gives a hand signal to the second man and then he either crosses the street or stops at a store window or slips into some alley. The second man takes his place. The first man finally falls behind the third detective. They continue to rotate until the surveillance is completed."

"Another thing," Joe put in. "If the suspect gets to a street intersection and makes a left or right turn or walks into a building, the first detective keeps right on walking. The next detective then makes the turn or follows the suspect into the building."

"That sounds easy," Chet commented.

Mr. Hardy laughed. "Yes, but you've got to be prepared for the unexpected. The suspect might jump into a bus or taxi. In that case, the second man tailing him gets into the bus or continues the surveillance by taxi. Always be sure you have enough money with you."

"What time do we start?" Frank asked, looking at his father.

"I suggest you station yourselves near the intersection where Lackey gets off the bus downtown. Be there about six-thirty P.M. Since he always goes home first, he won't show up until a quarter of seven at the earliest. Joe, you be the first shadow. Loiter nonchalantly as close to the bus stop as possible. Frank, you take the second spot, and Chet third. Is everything clear?"

"Yes," all three said excitedly.

"Will you be anywhere near us?" Chet asked.

"You bet," said Mr. Hardy. "I'll be in an unmarked police car with the Narcotics Bureau detectives. You're not to take any risks. I want you to remember this. If any of you sees that one of the other boys is in trouble, walk out into the street and hold both arms straight up in the air. We'll always be within sight of you."

"Okay," said Chet.

At six-thirty P.M. the trio arrived at the designated place and each boy stationed himself at a different spot. Two hours went by. Bus after bus discharged passengers, but Lackey was not among them. Finally the man alighted from one of the local buses. He stopped to light a cigarette and glanced up and down the street. Apparently satisfied that he was not being observed, he walked along the street at a moderate pace.

Joe, who had been idling on the bottom step of a nearby porch, went after him. Frank and Chet fell in line and followed. The radio police car was some distance behind Chet.

At the next intersection Lackey paused to tie a shoelace and looked around apprehensively. Joe walked past him and continued on. The suspect then made a right turn and Frank took up the surveillance. Joe fell in behind Chet later.

Lackey passed two more intersections, then stopped again. He lighted another cigarette while looking quickly up and down the street. He turned right again. Frank kept on going straight. It was Chet's turn to tail the man now!

Chet had been walking at a moderate pace and had not expected Lackey to change his speed. But when he arrived at the corner, he could not see Lackey and experienced a sickening feeling of failure. However, he realized that the man could not have gone far and signaled Joe to proceed to the corner.

Chet stopped in front of the third building on the block and listened. Hearing voices in the alleyway, he decided to investigate.

He signaled Joe to wait at the entrance of the alley. The building was old and dilapidated. Chinks of light filtered through holes in the shades. Chet tiptoed along the alley.

The voices he heard were now distinct. A man pleaded, "Give me some of the stuff! I need it quick, please! Don't stall, Lazar, you've got all the jewelry now!"

Chet recognized the speaker through a hole in the shade of the nearest window. *Ronald Lackey!* He was sitting at the kitchen table.

Then a raspy voice taunted, "Look at him, the big executive! He'll do anything we say for the stuff. We're going to own Towers soon! Okay, Dale, let him have a fix and keep him quiet."

"Easy, Ron. We'll take care of you." Chet figured it was Dale Britt speaking.

At that moment the boy moved so that he could see better through his peephole. As he did, he accidentally kicked an empty soda bottle, which broke with a crash. In trying to escape, he stumbled. Before he knew it, he was grabbed by two strong rough hands. He managed to yell for help before he was dragged into the kitchen.

Chet was knocked into a chair by a hairy thug. "What were you doing in the alley?" demanded the raspy-voiced man, whom Chet assumed was Lazar. "Make sure you tell the truth or I'll break every bone in your body!"

"Nothing," Chet replied shakily. "I was just going for a walk and got lost."

"Where do you live?" Britt asked sharply.

"I'm from out of town. Right now I'm staying with a friend on Ivy Hill Avenue. I came up to ask directions." Chet was desperately trying to stall for time, knowing that Joe would get help. "You see, if you could only tell me how to get to Pennsylvania Station, I could find my way—"

"You must be a stool pigeon!" the hairy thug rasped. "Now tell us the truth or we'll—"

Just then the alley door was smashed in by Mr. Hardy and two Narcotics Bureau detectives.

"The cops! Beat it!" Britt yelled. He raced toward

"The cops! Beat it!" Britt yelled

the front door but was stopped by Frank, Joe, and another narcotics detective, who promptly searched and handcuffed him. Then he was led back to the kitchen.

Lazar and Lackey sat handcuffed on chairs, the picture of dejection.

"Who's he?" Frank asked, pointing to the hairy thug.

"His name's Lazar," Lieutenant Wilson from the Narcotics Bureau explained. "He pulled a knife, but didn't get very far. He kept looking at the refrigerator and led us right to the evidence. We found a small .32 caliber automatic between two slices of bread. In the crisper were bags of heroin worth fifty thousand dollars on the retail market and hidden in the freezer was some very expensive jewelry."

As Lieutenant Wilson advised the three captives of their rights, Mr. Hardy said, "Now we just have to clear up the New York angle. How about giving us your story, Mr. Lackey?"

Lackey, who refused a lawyer, said he was willing to make a statement. "I know I won't get out of this," he said. "So I might as well tell you everything. I met Dale Britt just before I was made junior vice-president of Towers. Dale introduced me to smoking grass, and eventually to heroin.

"The more addicted I became the more money it cost. Britt thought I was wealthy, but soon I could not raise any more. Right after I told him this, he arranged a meeting with Lazar. Lazar agreed to furnish me with junk provided that I stole jewelry from Towers. He planned all the details of the theft."

Lackey mopped his brow and took a deep breath. "In the midst of the confusion during the fire, I went to Jerome Dempster's counter, dumped the contents of one tray into a paper bag, and put it in my pocket. Then I walked to the closet, pretending I wanted to help put out the fire. I threw the tray in the flames. Earlier I had tampered with the fire extinguisher so it wouldn't work. Then I ran outside, met Britt as prearranged, and handed him the bag.

"The next day he gave me a few gems as my share. I pawned them because I had a lot of debts."

Lackey, who had not had his promised fix, perspired and started to shake. "I can't do without the stuff!" he moaned. "Believe me, if I had known what I was getting into, I would have never touched it!"

"You'll have to come with us," Lieutenant Wilson said. "You'll be able to kick the habit, if you really want to. It'll be rough, but you'll get all the help possible."

Lackey nodded, and Lieutenant Wilson led him outside. His two accomplices were already in the police car.

Mr. Hardy and the boys said good-by to Lieutenant Wilson and the other detectives, then took a taxi to their hotel. On the way Chet said, "Lackey was sure in bad shape. I never saw a guy who needed a fix. What a horrible thing to be addicted to drugs!"

MORE DETAILS ABOUT SURVEILLANCE
IN CHAPTER XI, PAGE 188.

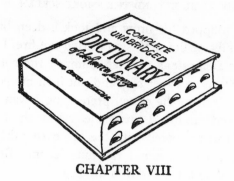

CHAPTER VIII

DICTIONARY FOR A DETECTIVE

Special Language of Criminals, Police Terminology

An expert detective must also be an expert in criminal slang. Members of the underworld have a language all their own, and an investigator who is not familiar with it cannot do his job effectively.

Suppose that a criminal is willing to make a statement at police headquarters and give an account of how a certain crime was committed. The detective who constantly interrupts him for explanations of his slang might irritate him to the point where it becomes impossible to obtain a clear, coherent story. Or if a detective is working undercover, he must talk in the same manner the criminals do in order not to arouse suspicion.

The following list of criminal slang expressions will give you some idea of what an investigator must know. Of course there are many more words and phrases—criminal slang varies in different parts of the country and changes constantly. A good detective must always be on the alert to learn new expressions.

SLANG OF CRIMINALS

action. Betting, wagering, gambling play.

artillery. Guns, weapons.

bag. To steal. (In police language to arrest. In narcotics slang a glassine bag of heroin.)

berries. Dollars.

big house. Penitentiary.

bit. Term in prison.

blast. Shoot.

blow. Leave hastily, run away.

book. Maximum sentence, as in "The judge threw the book at him." Also, a betting operation.

bouncer. A worthless check.

box. A safe.

box man. A safecracker.

brass. Fake jewelry.

bull. Police officer or detective.

bull buster. One who fights a policeman.

bunco. To cheat or swindle.

buried. Held incommunicado.

burn. To electrocute, to be electrocuted.

can. Prison.

cannon (or tool). Revolver or pistol. Also a pick-pocket who does actual stealing.

can opener. Safe ripper.

capper. A go-between for gamblers, one who leads victims into a gambling place.

carpet place. A high-class gambling place.

clean. Without funds. Not armed. No previous police record. Not in any way involved in the case being investigated.

clip. To steal from, as in "to clip a victim."

college. Penitentiary.

con. A convict. To swindle or persuade. To alibi on the spur of the moment.

contract. An agreement in the underworld to kill someone.

cooler. A prison or jail. Also a deck of cards, prepared for cheating at gambling.

coop. Jail, prison.

cop a plea. To plead guilty to a lesser charge, in order to escape penalty for more serious charge.

copper. Policeman.

copper-hearted. By nature a police informer.

creeper. Sneak thief.

croaker joint. Hospital.

crusher. Policeman.

cutter. District Attorney (D.A.).

czar. Principal warden of penitentiary.

damper. Cash register.

decoy. To entice, something that is not real or what it appears to be. Female accomplice of a gang of robbers. Police also use decoys to trap muggers.

dee-dee. Person pretending to be friendly.

dick. Detective or plainclothesman.

dip. Pickpocket.

doing it all. Serving a life sentence.

doughnut. Automobile tire.

drill. To shoot.

dropper. Paid killer.

dummy up. To become silent.

end. Share or portion of illegal gains.

enforcer. A strong-arm man who specializes in maiming or killing other criminals for gang bosses.

equalizer. Pistol or revolver.

erase. To kill.

fagin. An adult thief who teaches minors to steal and keeps the major portion of the loot.

fall. To be arrested.

fall money. Money for bail or lawyers.

fanning a sucker. Locating a victim.

fed. U. S. Officer. (Also: Uncle Sam, T-man.)

Federal beef. Federal offense.

fence. A person who buys and sells stolen goods.

fingerman. One who points out a victim.

fingers end. Ten percent of the loot.

fink. Traitor.

fix. To arrange, to make a deal; to secure a favor.

flatfoot. Policeman.

flattie. Policeman or detective.

frisk. To steal from a person, pickpocketing. (In police work to search a person for concealed weapons.)

front guy. Man with good appearance and personality.

fuzz. Policemen or detectives.

G. $1,000.

gat. Gun.

get to. To bribe.

G-man. Federal officer, particularly an FBI agent.

grab. To arrest; to kidnap.

grand. $1,000.

grease. To pay protection or tribute.

gumshoes. Detectives.

gun moll. A woman companion of a gunman or gangster; a female robber.

guzzled. Forced by painful methods to give information.

heater. Revolver or pistol.

heeled. Carrying a revolver or pistol.

heist. Robbery; a holdup; a theft.

herder. Guard in a penal institution.

hideout. Place of refuge to avoid arrest or capture.

hijacker. A person who robs or takes by force goods in transit.

hit. To kill. To make a "killing" or a big theft.

hole. Solitary confinement in prison.

hood. Hoodlum; strong-arm man; mugger, stickup man or killer.

hot. Stolen goods or a man wanted by police. (Also: sizzling, in a jam.)

hush money. A bribe paid to ensure silence.

ice. Diamonds.

in the bag. All set, okay, everything arranged.

iron. Gun.

Italian football. Bomb.

John. Sucker.

John Law. Police officer.

jugged. Arrested.

juiced. Electrocuted.

kale. Money.

kick. Pocket.

knowledge box. School.

kosher. Not guilty (see clean).

lam. To run or flee.

lamp. Eye.

laying paper. Passing worthless checks.

layout. Gambling or dope outfit.

lifeboat. A pardon.

lift. Steal.

lob. A sap.

mark. A victim of a confidence man.

mechanic. Skilled professional criminal.

moonlighter. Midnight prowler.

mouthpiece. Lawyer, especially a criminal lawyer.

mower. Machine gun.

mush. Mouth.

natural. Seven years' imprisonment.

nippers. Handcuffs. Leg irons.

nucks. Brass knuckles.

on the Erie. Someone listening.

on the spot. Marked for killing.

out. An alibi.

pad. Money for protection. Also living quarters.

paddy wagon. Police patrol wagon.

paper. Any kind of paper money, including checks.

paperhanger. Passer of counterfeit bills or bad checks.

pen. Penitentiary.

pew. Electric chair.

pigeon. A person who is, or lets himself be, easily tricked, especially in gambling.

pineapple. A bomb, generally a small bomb similar to a hand grenade.

queer. Counterfeit money.

queer shover. Passer of counterfeit money.

rap. Conviction. Prison sentence.

rap sheet. Arrest record.

rat. To inform on a fellow criminal. An informer.

rock. Any precious gem, generally a diamond.

rod. Pistol or revolver.

rub out. Kill.

runner. An agent of a bookmaker.

sing. Inform, squeal.

sleeper. Night watchman.

spring. To release from custody.

stool pigeon. Informer.

sugar. Money.

swag. Stolen property.

sweet pea. Easy victim.

take. Proceeds of illegal activity or consideration paid to police officers to overlook illegal activity.

tin. Police shield or badge.

tommy gun. A submachine gun. A "tommy man" is one who uses such a weapon.

torpedo. Paid killer.

triggerman. Gunman, especially a hired assassin.

typewriter. Submachine gun.

up. In jail. "Up the river."

useless. Dead.

weeper. A beggar who presents an elaborate sorrowful tale to get money.

wet goods. Stolen goods.

whiz. A pickpocket. To pick pockets.

wiper. A killer.

wired. Protected by burglar alarm. Also, political connections.

yard. $100.

zipper. To shut up or keep the mouth shut.

POLICE TERMINOLOGY

APB. All points bulletin.

book. Arrest, arrest record.

bug. Plant electronic listening device.

bust. Police breaking up a criminal operation, arrest.

collar. Arrest.

DOA. Dead on arrival (from the notations on hospital records).

fan. To locate, to search.

flier. Wanted notice.

frisk. Search for weapons on person.

kickback. Payoff to police officers to overlook criminal operations.

M.O. (modus operandi). Details of method used during the commission of a crime.

plant. The assignment of officers to keep a continuous watch on a place. "The police put a plant on the hideout." An object or a plan to trap a suspect.

rap sheet, record. A criminal record.

stakeout. The same as plant.

tag. To arrest.

tail. To follow; also a surveillant.

tip. A warning; information from an informant.

wiretapping. To electronically hear and/or record a telephone conversation.

CHAPTER IX

HIGH DANGER
Drug Abuse

Fans of the Hardy Boys no doubt have read much about the so-called drug culture and have been warned about its dangers. Drugs have invaded all social classes and age groups and the destructive effects are widespread. Almost invariably the addict will turn to crime to support his habit. It is, therefore, not only a threat to him but to society as well.

Law-enforcement officers working on narcotics cases often operate undercover. If spotted, they may face severe maiming or death. Drug dealers and addicts live in constant fear of detection and are suspicious of any outsider. The narcotics officer must be able to understand the particular language of the drug culture, be familiar with the various kinds of drugs, and be able to spot the symptoms of the users.

A list has been compiled to provide some understanding of the most common drugs, the slang words used for them, and the effect they have on people.

Some of these drugs are prescribed by physicians, and under certain circumstances are valuable medicines. However, it is not only illegal, but also irresponsible and dangerous to take them without a doctor's prescription.

The drugs most often abused are divided into six groups: narcotics, stimulants, sedatives, hallucinogens (psychedelics), marijuana, and organic solvents.

NARCOTICS

In this group are heroin, methadone, morphine, codeine, and cocaine. All are highly addictive and extremely dangerous. They produce lethargy, euphoria (high), constricted pupils, respiratory depression and loss of appetite and weight. Codeine abusers scratch themselves and seem to be intoxicated.

Addicts who inject narcotics can usually be identified by needle marks, scars, or abscesses at the injection sites. Often they will wear long-sleeved shirts even in the summer heat to hide those marks, and put on sunglasses indoors so that their constricted pupils cannot be noticed.

Withdrawal from narcotics is extremely difficult. They cause serious personality problems, possible criminal involvement, and bacterial diseases like hepatitis. Overdoses can result in convulsions and death. A reduction of fertility has also been noted.

Heroin: White or brownish powder usually sold in glassine bags or capsules. Bitter in taste, faint vinegar odor.

 Slang: H, Horse, Smack, Scag, Hard Stuff, Harry, Dope
 Method of use: Injected or sniffed
 Medical use: None

Morphine: White powder, tablets, capsules, or liquid. Bitter in taste and odorless.

 Slang: M, Morph, Miss Emma, White Stuff
 Method of use: Injected or taken orally
 Medical use: Strong pain reliever

Methadone: White tablets or liquid. Bitter in taste.

 Slang: Joke, Dollies
 Method of use: Oral, or by injection
 Medical use: Pain killer, cough depressant. Also given to heroin addicts in rehabilitation programs because it blocks addiction to heroin.

Codeine: White powder, tablets, or liquid. Bitter in taste. Used in some cough medicines.

 Slang: Syrup, Turps, Robo, Romo, Medicine
 Method of use: Oral
 Medical use: Pain killer, cough suppressant

Cocaine: White crystalline powder, bitter and odorless. Numbs lips and tongue. Sold in glassine bags or capsules.

    Slang: Coke, Snow, Happy Dust, Girl, Stardust
    Method of use: Sniffed or injected
    Medical use: Local anesthetic

STIMULANTS

Stimulants are addictive and very dangerous. They produce excitability, rapid and slurred speech, dry mouth and lips, bad breath, itchy nose, sweating, insomnia, hallucinations, and possible development of psychoses.

Amphetamines (Benzedrine and Biphetamine):
Heart-shaped pills, white and off-pink in color; or capsules. Odorless and bitter in taste.

    Slang: Bennies, Peaches, Hearts, Speed, Ups, Pep pills
    Method of use: Oral, or by injection
    Medical use: For weight reduction, mild depressions

Dextroamphetamines (Dexedrine, Synatan, and Appetrol): White—sometimes pink, heart-shaped tablet, also in capsule form. Odorless and bitter in taste.

    Slang: Dexies, Hearts, Speed, Ups, Footballs
    Method of use: Oral, or by injection
    Medical use: For weight reduction, mild depressions

Methamphetamines (Desoxyn, Methedrine, and Ambar) : Tablets, pink, white, and yellow in color, also in liquid form (glass vials). Odorless and bitter in taste.

> *Slang:* Meth, Monster, Speed, Wake-ups, Ups, Crystal
>
> *Method of use:* Oral, or by injection
>
> *Medical use:* For weight reduction, mild depressions

SEDATIVES

Sedatives are addictive. They produce a skin rash, slurred speech, nausea, dilated pupils. Constant use can lead to serious emotional disorder and memory loss. Brain damage is possible. In severe abuse, central nervous system becomes depressed and breathing stops, causing death.

Doriden: White tablets, chemical odor, bitter in taste.

> *Slang:* Cibas, Cibees, Gorilla pills, Goofballs, Downs
>
> *Method of use:* Oral, or by injection
>
> *Medical use:* Sleeping tablets and tension relievers

Seconal: Reddish-orange capsules, sometimes liquid. Odorless, bitter in taste.

> *Slang:* Reds, Red birds, Red devils, Goofballs, GB's, Downs
>
> *Method of use:* Oral, or by injection
>
> *Medical use:* Sleeping tablets and tension relievers

Tuinal: Red and blue capsules. Odorless, bitter in taste.

> *Slang:* Rainbows, Bullets, Christmas trees, Goofballs, GB's, Jolly beans, Downs
> *Method of use:* Oral
> *Medical use:* Sleeping tablets, tension relievers

Nembutal: Yellow capsules, tablets, and liquid. Odorless, bitter in taste.

> *Slang:* Yellow jackets, Yellow birds, Yellows, Nimbies, Candy, Goofballs, Downs, Yellow submarines
> *Method of use:* Oral, or by injection
> *Medical use:* Sleeping tablets, tension relievers

HALLUCINOGENS (Acids)

Hallucinogens are extremely dangerous mind-altering drugs. Users may appear in a trancelike state, show anxiety, confusion, often fear and terror. Perceptual changes involve senses of sight, sound, touch, body image and time. Users have been known to be driven to suicide; also there is possible chromosomal damage.

LSD (Lysergic Acid Diethylamide): White, crystalline powder, tasteless, odorless.

> *Slang:* Acid, Blue Cheer, Chief, Peace, Trips, Black Magic
> *Method of use:* Oral: Dissolved on cookies, sugar cubes, crackers. Or by injection.
> *Medical use:* None. Was used for psychiatric experimentation only.

STP (Dimethoxymethylamphetamine): White, crystalline powder, tasteless, odorless.
> *Slang:* Dom, Serenity, Tranquility, Peace
> *Method of use:* Same as LSD
> *Medical use:* None

DMT (Dimethyltryptamine): White, crystalline powder, tasteless, odorless.
> *Slang:* Acid
> *Method of use:* Same as LSD
> *Medical use:* None

MARIJUANA (Cannabis sativa)

Marijuana has a slight hallucinatory effect. It is a dangerous drug mainly because it leads to a drug environment and often to stronger drugs such as narcotics. The user may appear animated and hysterical, with rapid, loud talk, and bursts of laughter. Later the user may feel sleepy and stuporous. Depth perception is distorted. Eyes may appear red. Marijuana increases sensations present before the drug is taken, such as appetite, thirst, etc. Marijuana is the greenish-brown, coarsely-ground leaf of the Cannabis sativa plant. The smoke of marijuana smells a little like burning leaves or rope.

> *Slang:* Grass, Weed, Pot, Reefer, Hay, Locoweed, Hash
> *Method of use:* Usually smoked. Cigarettes are small with the paper tucked in at both ends. It can also be chewed, sniffed, smoked through a pipe, or baked into cookies.
> *Medical use:* None

ORGANIC SOLVENTS

Airplane glue, gasoline, aerosols, and cleaning fluids are among this group. They usually have a hydro-carbon taste and odor. They are very dangerous. Similar to alcohol intoxication, they cause slurred speech, red eyes and nostrils, ringing in ears, nausea and vomiting, hallucinations, blurred vision, poor coordination and respiratory depression. There is a possibility of brain damage.

Slang: Sniffing, Snorting, The Bag, Fluid
Method of use: Inhaled by use of paper and plastic bags. Sometimes poured on rags and handkerchiefs.
Medical use: None

COMMON TERMINOLOGY USED BY ADDICTS AND DEALERS

acidhead. Frequent user of LSD (Also: freak, cube-head.)
boost. Shoplift.
bread. Money. (Also: scratch, geetis, lettuce, long green, folding stuff.)
burned. A bad supply or swindle.
bust. Arrest. (Also: clip, glue, bat out, drop, mail, can, jug.)
cap. Capsule.
cat. Sharp character.
chip. Use small amounts of drugs irregularly. (Also: dabble, joy-pop.)

clean. Completely free of all drugs.

cokie. Cocaine addict.

cold turkey. To withdraw from drugs without help of medication.

connect. Purchase drugs. (Also: score, hit, make a meet, domino.)

connection. Dope peddler, source of narcotics. (Also: dealer, bit man, pusher, bagman.)

deck. Container of drugs. (Also: bindle, paper, bag, piece—usually a one-ounce package.)

dime bag. $10 package of narcotics.

dirty. Possessing drugs, liable to arrest if searched.

dripper. Eyedropper used in mainlining. (Also: gun.)

dummy. Poor-quality narcotics. (Also: flea powder, lemon, lemonade, Lipton tea, blank, turkey.)

dynamite. High-grade heroin.

fireplace ritual. In Synanon (see under S) terms, a dressing-down in presence of all residents who decide punishment.

fix. A drug injection, usually heroin. (Also: geezer.)

freakout. Bad experience with psychedelics; also a chemical high.

goofball addict. Person addicted to barbiturates.

gut level. Emotional depth.

haircut. In Synanon terms, a verbal dressing-down by one or more older members.

high. Under the influence of drugs. (Also: lit up, blasted, charged up, wasted, shot down, coasting, floating, banging, fixed, flying, leaping, belted, twisted, wired.)

hit the bricks. Released from jail. (Also: on the ground, on the street, fresh and sweet.)

hooked. Addicted. (Also: have a monkey on the back, strung out.)

hustle. In Synanon terms, gather food, clothing; in street language, to prostitute.

ice cream habit. A small, irregular habit. (Also: weekend habit, three-day habit.)

junk. Drugs, usually heroin.

junkie. A drug addict. (Also: hype, gow head, AD, hophead, junker.)

kick the habit. Stop using drugs. (Also: to fold up, hang up, make the turn.)

locked up. Imprisoned or hospitalized.

mainline. Inject heroin directly into the veins. (Also: jab, pop, bang, shoot up.)

manicure. Remove the dirt, seeds, and stems from marijuana.

methhead. Habitual user of methamphetamines.

nail. Needle. (Also: spike.)

narco. Narcotics detective.

nickel bag. $5 packet of narcotics.

on ice. In jail. (Also: slammed, doing a bit, boxed, behind the iron house, in the cooler.)

on the nod. Sleepy.

pad. Apartment where drugs are used. (Also: shooting gallery.)

pass. To transfer drugs.

pillhead. Users of barbiturates and amphetamines.

push. To sell narcotics. (Also: deal.)

script. Prescription. (Also: paper, reader.)

shoot dope. Take heroin.

shuck off. Fail to work effectively.

split. To quit Synanon.

square. A nonaddicted person. (Also: do-righter, apple, do-right John.)

Synanon. Form of leaderless group therapy.

tripping. Under the influence of a hallucinogen.

turned off. Withdrawn from drugs. (Also: washed up.)

vice squad. The ones who are clean.

works. Equipment for injecting drugs. (Also: biz, machinery, tools, factory, layout, artillery, gimmicks.)

weedhead. Marijuana smoker.

Not every drug and not every slang expression can be covered in this limited space. Also, the language differs in various areas and changes constantly. But this chapter will give readers an idea of the dangers of drug abuse, and what law-enforcement officers must know about illegal drug use.

INNOCENT UNTIL PROVED GUILTY

A Look at the Law

It is imperative for law-enforcement officers to be familiar with court procedures and legal terminology. After a crime has been investigated and the suspect apprehended, his guilt must be proved before a court of justice beyond a reasonable doubt.

The laws and the organization of the courts vary among the different states. Therefore it is not possible to describe legal procedure in criminal cases in detail. But the following will give you a general idea of our legal system.

Crimes are usually divided into two groups: misdemeanors and felonies. In some states, felonies are called high misdemeanors. Also there are offenses which are quasi-criminal in nature; for instance, traffic violations, violations of municipal ordinances, and breaches of the peace.

A felony is a serious crime, such as murder, robbery, arson, grand larceny, burglary, and so on. A misdemeanor is a lesser crime, such as petty larceny, purse snatching, conspiracy, assaults, and gambling.

The value of the property involved is normally used to classify a crime. For example, in some states the theft of money or property of fifty dollars and more is grand larceny and a felony, while the theft of money or property under fifty dollars is petty larceny and a misdemeanor. It follows that the penalty for a felony is greater than for a misdemeanor.

A person can be arrested only when a crime has been committed. Arrests can be made by two methods: by warrant or by legal authority.

By warrant. Anyone having knowledge that a crime has been committed may go before a judge or clerk of the court and sign a written complaint charging a person with that specific crime. Only then will the judge issue the warrant for arrest. A warrant directs the police to arrest the person named in it and arraign him before a court, which means to bring him before the judge so that he may answer the charge against him.

By legal authority. Arrests may be made by a police officer without a warrant whenever he sees a crime or quasi crime committed. He may also arrest without a warrant when he has probable cause to believe that a felony has been committed not in his presence.

The same goes for a private citizen. However, citizen's arrests are rare, mainly because if private citizens make a mistake they can be sued more easily than police officers can.

After arrest a suspect is brought before a lower court so he can be arraigned. These courts differ in name in the various jurisdictions, such as: municipal court, sessions court, or magistrate's court. They have the power to try only quasi crimes and misdemeanors, where there is no right to a trial by jury.

In all other cases they may conduct only a preliminary hearing. The purpose of such a hearing is not to decide whether the defendant (the suspect) is guilty, but merely to determine if there is enough evidence to have the case examined by the Grand Jury. If the judge decides there is not enough evidence, the defendant is released. If, however, he feels that there is enough evidence, the defendant is bound over to the Grand Jury and bail is set. A defendant may refuse to have this preliminary hearing and waive his right in favor of the prosecutor presenting the case to the Grand Jury directly.

The Grand Jury is not a trial jury. It is appointed by various methods in different states and decides whether or not there is sufficient evidence to bring the accused to trial. A Grand Jury may either report "no bill," in which case the accused is released, or it may find a "true bill" and draw up an indictment. This is a formal charge specifying the violation of the law for which the accused must stand trial.

During the time a defendant is awaiting trial in any court, or an investigation by the Grand Jury, he may either be kept in jail or be set free on bail. This means that he puts up a sum of money, bond, or guarantee in the amount specified by the judge which will be forfeited if the accused does not appear for trial. In most states the courts will allow bail on almost any charge except murder.

A defendant may plead guilty at any time. He may even waive indictment by the Grand Jury and plead guilty. If he elects trial, he may waive trial by the Petit Jury (a jury of twelve persons that sits at civil and criminal trials to try and decide finally on the facts at issue) and elect to stand trial before a judge alone. If found guilty, he is sentenced to punishment by the judge. The judge may imprison him for a certain length of time and/or fine him a sum of money, or give him a suspended sentence and place him on probation for a specific time.

The convicted person may always appeal a decision to the next higher court.

Following are brief definitions of the more common legal terms:

abet. To encourage another to commit a crime.
accomplice. One who is involved in the commission of a crime with others.
acquit. A finding by a jury that the prosecution has not proved the guilt of a defendant beyond a reasonable doubt.

alias (A-lee-us). An assumed name.

corpus delicti (KOR-pus duh-LIK-tye). The basic facts constituting a crime. This is often mistakenly thought to mean the body of a murder victim.

duress. Unlawful influence to force compliance, physically or mentally.

ex parte. On or from one side only, from a one-sided point of view.

ex post facto. After the fact. Affecting what has happened before.

habeas corpus. An order from a court to produce a prisoner in court so that the legality of the detention may be decided.

indict (in-DYT). To accuse of a crime, in writing, by a Grand Jury.

Miranda Ruling. The U. S. Supreme Court on June 13, 1966, made public its decision following its review in the case of *Miranda v. Arizona.*

In simple terms, the decision was that before an arrested person could be questioned by law-enforcement officers he must be advised of his constitutional rights. Any statement he makes without being advised of these rights cannot be used against him in court. The rights are:

1. To remain silent. Anything the suspect says can be used against him in court.
2. To consult a lawyer for advice before questioning, and to have the lawyer present during questioning.

3. If the suspect cannot afford a lawyer, the court will appoint one for him before questioning if he so desires.

4. If the suspect wishes to answer questions without a lawyer present, he can stop answering at any time until he consults a lawyer.

The arrested person can waive these rights either orally or in writing. Most law-enforcement agencies use a printed form that the arrested person is requested to sign as evidence that he was properly advised. It also contains a waiver of rights paragraph which he signs if he wishes to.

recidivist (re-SID-ih-vist) . A repeater in crime.

subpoena (suh-PEE-nuh) . A written order to appear in court.

venue (VEN-yoo) . The place (county) where the trial is held.

waive. To give up a legal right.

CHAPTER XI

THE SUSPECT AND HIS SHADOW

Secret Watch

SURVEILLANCE comes from the French word *surveiller* meaning "to watch."

It is the secret observation of persons, places, or things. Some call it spy work. In police work its objectives are:

To apprehend a person by watching his home and places or persons he is known to visit.

To obtain information on a suspect and his associates:

Habits
Daily routine
Persons contacted
Place of employment
Home address, floor, apartment number
Transportation used
To obtain evidence of a crime
To obtain basis for a search warrant
To catch a suspect in a criminal act
To prevent commission of a crime

Fixed Surveillance

Sometimes called a plant or stakeout. A fixed surveillance is generally of a house or place of business. Arrangements should be made to cover all exits. Usually the best place for a fixed surveillance is in a room or office directly across the street from the exit being watched. Sometimes, if circumstances permit, an automobile is used.

Foot Surveillance

This is probably used most often. The number of men involved depends on various factors, such as the neighborhood in which the surveillance will take place, its purpose, and the availability of officers. Foot surveillance is usually conducted by one, two, or three men. In special cases, additional men may be used.

One-Man Surveillance

The subject is followed on foot in many cases. It is

SUSPECT TURNS A CORNER

SUSPECT TURNS CORNER
SURVEILLANT A
CROSSES STREET
SURVEILLANT B
FOLLOWS SUSPECT
SURVEILLANT C
FOLLOWS B
SURVEILLANT D
FOLLOWS C

WHERE CASE IS
IMPORTANT, AN
EXTRA SURVEILLANT
MAY BE PLACED IN
POSITION D

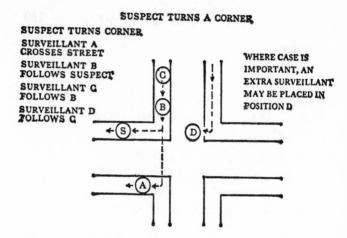

SUSPECT CONTINUES STRAIGHT AHEAD

S SUSPECT

A SURVEILLANT
IN POSITION A

B SURVEILLANT
IN POSITION B

C SURVEILLANT
IN POSITION C

D SURVEILLANT
IN POSITION D

When suspect turns corner, detective A crosses street,
B follows suspect, C follows B, D follows C.

When suspect continues straight ahead, detectives A,
B, and C remain in position behind him, D follows
across the street.

difficult for one officer to follow a subject for any extended length of time, or very closely, without running the risk of being detected.

However, many detectives become very efficient at this type of surveillance, particularly in large cities and crowded areas where the number of people walking serve as cover.

Two-Man Surveillance

This type has advantages over the one-man surveillance because the subject usually can be followed more closely and for longer periods of time. The risk of losing the subject is less and the surveillants are not as easily detected.

The first detective will follow the subject. He in turn is followed by the second detective. In some instances, the second man will parallel the subject slightly to his rear on the opposite side of the street. In an area of stores, he can usually follow the subject's movements by watching his reflection in windows.

The second man must always be alert to the possibility of a counter-surveillance by the cohorts of the subject.

Three-Man Surveillance

The subject on foot is followed by officer A, who, in turn, is followed by officer B. The function of B is to see if there is any counter-surveillance as well as to take over if officer A becomes conspicuous. Officer C is effectively used in this situation on the opposite side of the street. He can take up the tail if the subject turns a corner or makes a sudden stop allowing A and B to continue on past the subject in order to avoid detection. These officers can then back up C by reversing roles.

Automobile Surveillance

Whether or not a foot surveillance, an automobile surveillance, or a combination of both is used will be dictated by the habits and behavior of the subject.

If he is known to ride a car, bus, or taxi, a foot surveillance will be backed up by an automobile. This car can pick up one or two of the surveillants and follow the subject's vehicle until he alights. Then foot surveillance can continue. If possible, officer C will ride on a public conveyance with the subject for uninterrupted surveillance and observe any contacts which he might make.

Automobile surveillance should, if possible, be conducted with two radio cars and two men each, so that a second man can take up a foot surveillance if the subject leaves his vehicle, and also take notes during the car tail. A one-car tail job is subject to the same limitations as a one-man foot surveillance.

If two cars are used, car A will follow immediately behind the subject's car, if circumstances of the surveillance and traffic conditions permit. Often one or two intervening cars are allowed between the subject's car and car A. Car B will back up car A, and, when advisable, take the lead position during the surveillance.

In an important case, additional cars may be as

signed to the surveillance. They will at times bracket the subject's car by traveling on parallel streets. If the subject's car makes a turn, one of these cars can pick it up at the first intersection and continue the tail as car A.

Such maneuvers depend upon well-coordinated radio control from the lead car. Many times such transmissions are in simple code designed to confuse the suspect if he should be tuned in.

Tight Surveillance

A close physical tailing of the subject so that he is not lost is called tight surveillance. In some instances the subject is deliberately made aware of the tail as a form of psychological pressure. This might be done to prevent him from making a particular contact, or to force his hand. It usually causes him to panic and make a move that will provide information to the tailing officer.

Loose Surveillance

This is used when it is vital that the subject remain unaware of the tail. This method of surveillance is conducted at greater distances and dropped immediately if the subject seems to get suspicious.

Progressive Surveillance

This is staged over a period of time, if possible, depending on the nature of the case. For example: A businessman is suspected to be a fence. The police will set up a stakeout to cover his place of business. In addition to that he may be followed from his home to the train station, to determine where he parks his car, what contacts he makes, if any, what train he takes and where he usually sits.

Having established this pattern, a surveilling officer will board the same train at a later date, probably at the station before the subject's. He will sit in the rear of the car used by the subject, so he can observe any contacts, also at what station the subject leaves the train. Another officer will pick up the subject at the station and follow him to his place of business.

The subject will be tailed during the day if he leaves his business location, and on his return home at night. All persons the subject contacts during the day will be checked out, and if deemed advisable, they will be tailed.

Duties

The duties of an officer on surveillance will be guided by the objective. However, good investigative techniques dictate that he will:

Familiarize himself with all details of the case, including all persons involved, their descriptions, dress, habits, locations of homes and places frequented, personal contacts, transportation used, and neighborhoods in which they will most likely operate.

Maintain contact with the officer in charge of the investigation and promptly report by radio, telephone, hand signals, or messenger all pertinent developments.

Maintain detailed individual notes for the entire period of the surveillance from which logs or reports may be prepared. Notes and reports must show the specific time and place of each observation, the names of persons and places contacted, or physical descriptions and specific addresses.

Transportation used, such as bus, train, or plane, should be identified by company route and number. Automobiles should be identified by make, year, model, color, license plate number, and any special characteristics like trim, dents, etc.

Tips for Tailing

The surveillant should dress for the neighborhood to avoid looking out of place.

Prepare his mind for any eventuality. For example, if anyone asks what he is doing in the area, he must be prepared to give a good cover story.

Act as if he belongs in that area.

Watch out for a "check tail." Sometimes the criminal element may have someone following and observing him.

Always prepare visible signals with his partners in advance.

Always have money and change ready for any eventuality. He might need change in a hurry to telephone headquarters, or money for taxis and buses.

Always have an alternate plan ready if he loses his subject.

Conclusion

The art and importance of surveillance in the field of investigation cannot be stressed too highly. It is a technique used at almost every level of police work, and an officer trained in this art is considered a valuable asset to his organization.

CHAPTER XII

NO TWO OF THEM ALIKE
Visible and Latent Fingerprints

FINGERPRINTING is the principal means of positive identification for human beings. Of the millions of persons fingerprinted to date no two have ever been found to have even one fingerprint identical.

All fingerprints of criminals taken in the United States are sent to the FBI Identification Division in Washington. This division, established July 1, 1924, by an act of Congress, has fingerprint cards for almost one hundred million persons on file. It contains not only fingerprints of criminals, but also of military personnel, applicants for federal jobs, aliens, prisoners of war, civilians who have access to secret or classified information, and prints filed voluntarily by citizens for personal identification. It acts as a clearing house of arrest information for all the law-enforcement agencies in the United States and cooperates with more than eighty foreign countries in the exchange of criminal identifying data.

While fingerprint identification is a comparatively new science, it has been found that the ancient Chinese used thumb impressions on important documents, some of which are still in existence today. They were sealed, or signed, by the application of a thumbprint.

If you examine the inside surface of the tips of your fingers, you will see patterns formed by the ridges of your skin. These can be seen better through a magnifying glass.

By pressing your fingers against a piece of polished glass, the patterns formed by the ridges will show up clearly on the glass. At first they may look alike, but if you study them closely, you will note a variety of differences. With training and experience, you can discern these differences quickly.

One of the first men to discover that the ridge patterns of fingerprints differed was Marcello Malpighi, an Italian professor of anatomy, in the year 1686, but he did not follow up his discovery. In 1823 another professor of anatomy, John E. Purkinje of Germany, wrote a book on the subject.

Sir William Herschel, a British government officer stationed in Bengal, India, and Henry Faulds, a doctor in Tokyo, Japan, made further contributions in 1877 and 1880 respectively. They recommended that these patterns be used to identify people, but did not pursue their recommendations.

The next man of importance in fingerprinting was

the noted English scientist Sir Francis Galton. He made a study of the patterns and developed a system of classifying fingerprints. Sir Edward R. Henry, who later became chief commissioner of the London Metropolitan Police, was appointed to head a committee in 1898 to develop a practical method of classifying and filing fingerprints. He worked out a system, based on the Galton classification, which was henceforth known as the Henry System, and was adopted by Scotland Yard in 1901.

The Henry System has been refined and modified since then and is used in the United States and in all English-speaking countries.

There are other parts of the human body from which a fingerprint expert can make a positive identification. They are the palms of the hands and the soles of the feet. Most hospitals today take footprints of newborn babies to make certain the infants are given to the right mothers.

The friction ridge patterns on the palmar areas of the hand and the soles of the feet never change. They are developed before birth and remain the same until decomposition after death. Some criminals, such as the notorious John Dillinger, who was slain by the FBI in 1934, have tried to change or obliterate their fingerprints by burning their fingertips with acid. Others have used different means, but enough characteristics always remain for identification.

Fingerprints are classified and filed rather than palm prints or footprints because they are most often left at crime scenes. Also, they can be classified and filed more readily.

Fingerprint patterns are divided into three general groups: arches, loops, and whorls. These groups are subdivided as follows:

ARCHES	LOOPS
Plain Arch	Radial Loop
Tented Arch	Ulnar Loop

WHORLS
Plain Whorl
Central Pocket Loop Whorl
Double Loop Whorl
Accidental Whorl

Before the different type patterns are discussed, it will be necessary to understand some of the terms used in fingerprint work. The ridges and ridge formations that are commonly encountered are:

RIDGES

ENDING RIDGE

A ridge that ends abruptly.

FIGURE 1

BROKEN RIDGE

A ridge with a definite break or breaks in it, which, if joined, would form a continuous ridge.

FIGURE 2

FIGURE 3

EIGHT BASIC FINGERPRINT PATTERNS

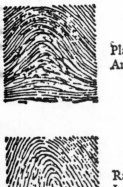 Plain Arch

 Tented Arch

 Radial* Loop

 Ulnar* Loop

 Plain Whorl

 Central Pocket Loop Whorl

 Double Loop Whorl

 Accidental Whorl

*These two patterns are classified as radial and ulnar loops if they appear in the left hand. If the prints were taken from the right hand, their classification would be reversed. (See pages 208-212 for discussion of loops, arches, and whorls.)

DOT

A dot is considered a ridge if its diameter is as great as the width of the surrounding ridges.

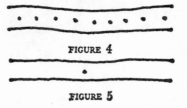

FIGURE 4

FIGURE 5

BIFURCATION

The point at which a single ridge forks or divides into two or more branches.

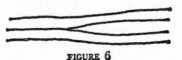

FIGURE 6

ISLAND

The formation caused by a bifurcation, the forks of which rejoin and continue as a single ridge.

FIGURE 7

SHORT RIDGE

A ridge whose length is materially shorter than surrounding ridges.

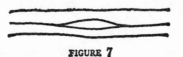

FIGURE 8

COMMON TYPES OF RIDGE FORMATIONS

ANGLE

The center ridge is regarded as forming a definite angle if the inside angle is 90° or less.

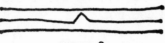

FIGURE 9

UPTHRUST

The center ridge is regarded as forming an upthrust if it rises at 45° or more from the horizontal plane (the ridge under it).

FIGURE 10

LOOPING RIDGE

A ridge that enters on either side of the fingerprint, recurves and leaves or tends to leave on the same side.

FIGURE 11

SHOULDERS OF LOOPING RIDGE

The shoulders of a looping ridge are located by drawing an imaginary line across the loop where the recurving portion of the ridge starts and ends. The shoulders are those points on the ridge cut by the imaginary line.

A ridge is considered a looping ridge when it has sufficient recurve. That means the ridge must cut or touch the shoulder line. Figures 12 and 13 meet the test. Figure 14 does not.

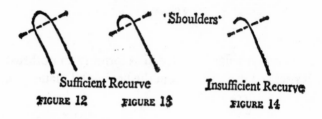

Sufficient Recurve   Insufficient Recurve

FIGURE 12   FIGURE 13   FIGURE 14

RECURVING RIDGES

Recurving ridges make a complete circuit and may be spiral, circular, or any variation of a circle.

FIGURE 15

PATTERN AREA

The pattern area is that part of a loop or whorl in which appear the cores, deltas, and ridges by which the fingerprint is classified. Type lines enclose the pattern area.

TYPE LINES

Type lines are defined as the two innermost ridges that start parallel, diverge, and surround or tend to surround the pattern area.

Figures 16 and 17 illustrate type lines and pattern areas in loop formations.

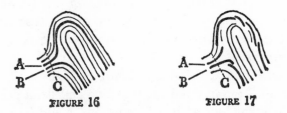

FIGURE 16   FIGURE 17

The ridges shown as *A* and *B* in Figures 16 and 17 are type lines. The point of divergence, or where they begin to separate, is shown by dotted line *C*. The area enclosed by the type lines is the pattern area.

Note that in these two illustrations there are other ridges that run parallel and diverge. They may not be called type lines because they are not the innermost ridges; only ridges *A* and *B* fit the definition for type lines.

Type lines are located in whorl patterns in the same manner. The only difference is that there are two sets of type lines, one on each side of the fingerprint.

It is very uncommon to find type lines which are continuous ridges, such as those shown in Figure 16. A typical pair of type lines would appear as in Figure 17; the rule is that when a type line has a definite break in it or ends abruptly, the next outer ridge is used as a type line.

DELTA

The delta is a reference point used in the classification of both loop and whorl type patterns.

A delta is defined as that point on a ridge at or nearest to the point of divergence of two type lines, and located at or directly in front of the point of divergence.

Some typical deltas are shown in Figures 18, 19, and 20. Bear in mind the type line and delta definitions as you look at these illustrations. *A* and *B* signify the type lines.

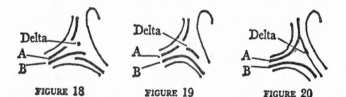

FIGURE 18   FIGURE 19   FIGURE 20

LOOP PATTERNS

A loop is that type of fingerprint pattern in which one or more of the ridges enter on either side of the fingerprint, recurve, touch or pass an imaginary line drawn from the delta to the core and pass out or tend to pass out on the side from which such ridge or ridges enter.

The core of a loop pattern is a reference point. It is always located on or within the recurve of the innermost looping ridge. Shown in Figure 21. The precise location of the core will vary depending on the appearance of other ridges within the recurve.

If there are no ridges within the innermost loop, the core is placed on the shoulder away from the delta. Indicated in Figure 22.

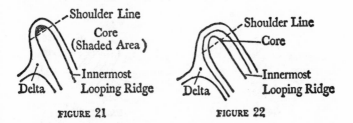

Ridges sometimes appear within the innermost looping ridge. If such a ridge comes up to the shoulder line or higher, the core is placed at the top of the ridge, as in Figures 23, 24, and 25.

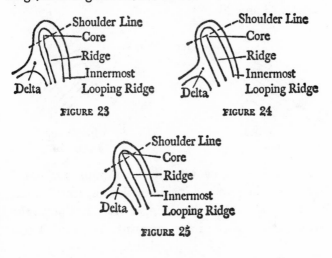

On occasion such a ridge will run through the recurve, which spoils the recurve, and the next looping ridge becomes the innermost looping ridge, as in Figure 26.

The tip of the ridge appearing within the innermost looping ridge of Figure 27 cannot be used as the core because it does not rise to the shoulder line.

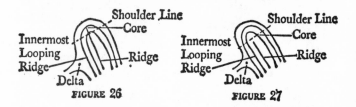

FIGURE 26   FIGURE 27

RADIAL AND ULNAR LOOPS

The only difference between the radial and ulnar loop patterns is the direction in which the looping ridges slant, commonly called the line of flow. See Figures 28 and 29.

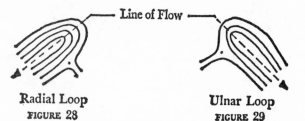

Radial Loop   Ulnar Loop
FIGURE 28   FIGURE 29

Radial loops flow toward the thumb (or radial bone, the bone on the inside of the forearm). Ulnar loops flow toward the little finger (or ulnar bone, the one on the outside of the forearm). You must know which hand a specific print is from in order to determine what kind of loop it is. Figure 28, a print taken from the right hand, would be a radial loop, and Figure 29 an ulnar loop. If, however, these patterns appeared in the left hand, their classification would be reversed.

The best way to determine which type of loop a certain print is, is to refer to the plain impressions at the bottom of the standard fingerprint card and to see which hand the print is from.

The essentials of a loop are:

A sufficient recurve
A delta
A ridge count across a looping ridge

Sufficient recurve and deltas have been discussed previously. In order to see if the third essential, a ridge count across a looping ridge, is present, an imaginary line must be drawn from the delta to the core and must cross or touch at least one recurving ridge. Figures 30 and 31 illustrate this. Figure 32 illustrates a fingerprint that has a delta, core, and recurving ridge. This print may not be classified as a loop because the recurving ridge is not crossed or touched by the imaginary line between delta and core.

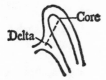

FIGURE 30

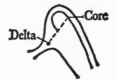

FIGURE 31

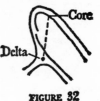

FIGURE 32

Most loop patterns will have more than one looping ridge. Each ridge crossed or touched by the imaginary line drawn between delta and core is counted. The delta and core are not counted.

ARCHES

PLAIN ARCH

In the plain arch pattern the ridges enter from one side, make a rise or curve in the center, and flow or tend to flow out on the other side. Figures 33 and 34 illustrate plain arch patterns.

Plain Arch
FIGURE 33

Plain Arch
FIGURE 34

TENTED ARCH

The tented arch pattern resembles a plain arch but possesses either an angle, an upthrust, or two of the three basic characteristics of a loop, as shown in Figures 35, 36, and 37.

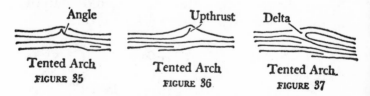

Angle

Tented Arch
FIGURE 35

Upthrust

Tented Arch
FIGURE 36

Delta

Tented Arch
FIGURE 37

In Figure 37 there is a looping ridge with sufficient recurve. The delta would be placed at the center of the recurve. As a result, there would be no ridge count across a recurving ridge. (See also Figure 32.)

WHORLS

PLAIN WHORL

A plain whorl, as shown in Figures 38 and 39, consists of one or more ridges that make a complete circuit, with two deltas. If an imaginary line is drawn between the deltas, at least one recurving ridge is cut or touched.

Plain Whorl
FIGURE 38

Plain Whorl
FIGURE 39

CENTRAL POCKET LOOP WHORL

A central pocket loop whorl, as shown in Figures 40 and 41, consists of at least one recurving ridge, or an obstruction at right angles to the line of flow. It has two deltas. When an imaginary line is drawn between the two, no recurving ridge within the pattern area is cut or touched.

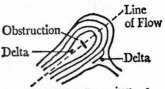

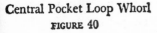
Central Pocket Loop Whorl
FIGURE 40

Central Pocket Loop Whorl
FIGURE 41

DOUBLE LOOP WHORL

A double loop consists of two separate loop formations, with two separate and distinct sets of shoulders and two deltas, as in Figure 42.

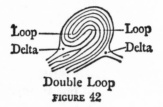

Double Loop
FIGURE 42

ACCIDENTAL WHORL

An accidental whorl consists of a combination of two or more different types of patterns with the exception of the plain arch. This exception is necessary, as every type pattern has ridges above and below the pattern area which conform to the arch definition.

The following are illustrations of accidental whorls. Figure 43 shows a loop over a tented arch, and Figure 44 shows a loop over a plain whorl.

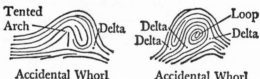

Accidental Whorl
FIGURE 43

Accidental Whorl
FIGURE 44

FINGERPRINT IDENTIFICATION

Each fingerprint card bearing the inked impression of all ten fingers of an arrested person is classified upon receipt at the FBI and police department identification divisions. This composite classification is a combination of an alphabetical and numerical formula applied to each of the ten fingerprints on the card. It serves as a filing index.

Fingerprint cards for many people who have similar but not identical prints bear the same classification and are filed together.

It is the responsibility of the technician to classify each card received and to compare the ridge details of the prints on it with those of all the cards filed under that classification. If he finds a card on file with the same ridge detail (ending ridges, bifurcations, islands, or dots) in exactly the same position as on the card he received, he has made an identification.

Latent fingerprint identification is made in the same manner as described above; that is, by painstaking comparison of ridge detail in the latent print. However, latent prints are not always complete, and sometimes identification must be made from just a fragment of one finger. For purposes of testimony in court, it is called the *unknown* print, since the person who left it at a crime scene is usually not known until the print has been identified with one on file with a law-enforcement agency. The print on file of a person arrested previously is referred to as the *known* print.

Having made an identification of an unknown print with a known print, the expert prepares photographic enlargements of each. He carefully marks and identifies all similarities. When he has found enough points of similarity in the known and unknown prints, he has made an identification and may testify in court to this effect. It is not necessary to establish a specific number of points of identity. However, the more of them the expert can identify, the more weight his testimony will carry.

Although many thousands of criminal cases have been solved by identifying latent fingerprints left at a crime scene, this technique has been beneficial in other areas as well.

The FBI Disaster Squad has frequently identified victims of airplane crashes and other disasters by obtaining latent fingerprints left by them on personal effects at their homes or places of employment. Latent prints were used in these instances as the victims had never been fingerprinted for employment, military service, or for criminal activity.

For those readers who have been stimulated to learn more about the science of criminal investigation, other areas of knowledge are available. Local police headquarters invite queries and inspection by young people. For readers in the New York City area, the world-famous Police Academy is a treasure of information, and the Federal Bureau of Investigation in Washington, D.C., conducts regular tours of its Identification Division and laboratory facilities.